ONCE UPON A
MOONLIT PATH

AVA STONE

ONCE UPON A
MOONLIT PATH

AVA STONE

DEDICATION

To the lovely Cass Dixon. Thank you so much for allowing me the use of your name and of Oscar's. ~ Ava

CHAPTER 1

Outskirts of Bocka Morrow, Cornwall ~ October, 1811

*E*ven from a distance, Castle Keyvnor seemed slightly terrifying. Perhaps it was the way the dark clouds seemed to hover over the turrets as a warning to travelers, or perhaps it was the spooky tales Lady Cassandra Priske had heard over the years about the place – tales of smuggling and witchcraft and of the castle's many ghosts. Just the thought of those tales made her slide a little closer to her sister on the bench and avert her gaze from the approaching medieval castle.

"There's no reason to squish me." Samantha glanced from her book with a slight frown, her red hair bouncing about her shoulders.

"Sorry." Cassy moved back toward the carriage window, though she was determined not to peer outside until after they'd arrived at the castle. "It does look frightening though, doesn't it?"

"Not this again," Papa complained. "It's *just* a sennight, Cassandra. Certainly you can survive a sennight."

Across the coach, Mama shook her head as though her patience had been lost for quite some time, and it probably had. While Cassy would love to plead her case one more time, that there was no reason for all of them to travel to southern Cornwall for the reading of Great-uncle Banfield's will in an ominous castle with an unfortunate past, the fact of the matter was she'd pled that case before they'd left Widcombe Hall and many times since, and her parents had yet to relent.

"Grandmama's brother lived there his whole life," Samantha said, reaching for Cassy's hand. "It can't be that frightening, now, can it?"

It was nice of her younger sister to try and soothe her worries, even if her worries couldn't be soothed. Cassy had, after all, been plagued with the worst fears ever since they'd received that summons from Banfield's solicitor, Mr. Hunt.

"Yes, but now that he's dead," their youngest brother Tobias began, his brow wiggling dramatically, "his ghost is just waiting for you to walk though the gates so he can *murder* you."

Papa slid his arm behind Mama and thumped Toby on the back of his head. "Leave your sister alone."

"Sorry, Father," Toby mumbled, sounding contrite, but he still had a wicked glint in his brown eyes like he was plotting something nefarious. Cassy and Samantha had been cursed with the worst little brothers in all the world. At least Alexander was still at Eton and they weren't plagued with both of them at the moment. Though she'd have been happy if their oldest brother Benjamin was with them, as he had always been her champion.

Toby stuck out his tongue at her, so Cassy kicked his ankle as he was sitting directly across from her. Of course the swift movement woke Oscar from his sleep at her feet, and the little poodle let out a startled bark.

"I'm sorry, sweet boy," she said and patted a spot on the bench between her and her sister. "Here come sit by us."

Oscar shook his black tail and then leapt onto the bench, squeezing himself between the two of them. A moment later, he rested his head on Cassy's lap and she petted the top of his head. At least she'd have her sweet dog with her for this journey.

"You should probably keep Oscar with you the whole time we're at Keyvnor," her brother laughed. "Maybe his ferocious bark will scare all the ghosts away from you."

"Toby!" Papa thumped him in the back of the head again. "Leave your sister alone."

"She kicked me."

"Cassandra, leave your brother alone. Honestly, the next one of you that annoys the other I'll have drawn and quartered once we arrive."

Samantha turned up her nose at the suggestion. "I hardly think you need to resort to such barbarism."

Papa narrowed his eyes on her. "Do not test my patience, Samantha," he bit out.

And, truly, Papa's patience had been rather thin ever since they'd left Somerset. Of course, if he'd just left the rest of them at Widcombe Hall he'd still have his patience and she wouldn't be subjected to Castle Keyvnor; but Cassy resisted the urge to say as much, however, and the rest of the short journey through the Cornish seaside village was spent in complete silence, with the exception of Oscar's cheerful panting.

Once Papa turned his attention away, Toby crossed his eyes and stuck his tongue out again. Oh, she would dearly love to kick the little villain once more and would be quite pleased if Papa *did* have her brother drawn and quartered once they arrived at Castle Keyvnor. Of course, as bad as

Toby was in the flesh he'd probably be even worse as one of Keyvnor's many spirits.

"It doesn't look so awful," Samantha whispered once they'd arrived and stood inside the medieval castle's courtyard. "Some might even call it charming."

Charming it was not. There was something about the place that made a chill race down Cassy's spine. She glanced up at the ancient castle and in one of the windows, she spotted a dark figure glaring down at them. "*He* looks awful," she muttered in response.

"Who?" Samantha frowned at her.

Cassy gestured to the fellow in the window. "That man right there. A perfectly horrid looking man in a perfectly horrid place. Probably some grave robber or something, all in black like—"

Her sister heaved a sigh. "I think you're imagination has run away with you again."

So perhaps he wasn't a grave robber. He was probably some distant relative here for the will reading, but he *did* look perfectly horrid. Samantha couldn't argue that. "Well, then, who do you think he is?"

Her sister shook her head. "I have no idea who you're talking about."

"The man right there in the window." Cassy pointed again, but this time there was no one there. Heavens! What in the—

Oscar growled at something and then bolted past Cassy and Samantha toward an open doorway.

"Oscar!" she yelled after him.

"Cassandra, do keep an eye on that beast," Papa complained as he stepped from the castle and back into the courtyard along with the Banfield butler.

～

*J*ack Hazelwood, Lord St. Giles, lined up his shot, struck his ball and bit back a smile as it bounced off the far end of the billiard table and rolled back toward him, stopping only an inch away from the baulk cushion. He stood up straight and glanced over his shoulder at Lord Michael Beck. "Your shot. Try not to hit my ball."

His friend glowered in return. "I'm not sure why I even play with you."

"You like the challenge?" Jack suggested, as Michael had never once even come close to beating him at this game.

"Must be it," his friend agreed as he approached the billiard table and lined up his own shot. After a moment of inspecting the table, he added, "I think the only way I could possibly win the lag is if the ghosts of Keyvnor guide my ball past yours somehow."

"It's just the lag," Jack replied, making his way to a chair a few feet away. If history had taught him anything, Michael would toil over his shot for more time than was necessary. "There's still lots of game to play after the first shot."

Michael snorted as he bent over the table. "Perhaps if I was playing against someone else. No—" he shook his head "—better hope some old ancestor will take pity on me."

"You and Lancaster have both lost your minds." Jack couldn't help but laugh. "The place hardly seems haunted, Michael." And it didn't. Castle Keyvnor was an old castle to be sure, mid-11th Century if he was judging the place correctly, but it just seemed like any other castle Jack had visited in the past. Cold stone walls, rounded turrets and old tapestries hung up in nearly every room, and—

"A lot of people have died here over the last several centuries," Michael replied as he finally took the shot with his cue stick.

Something his friend had said a number of times during

their trip from Newmarket along with Teddy Lockwood and Viscount Blackwater. "Name me one place in England where that isn't true." Jack released a sigh. "From the Roman centurions to the plague to more wars than I can count. There isn't one corner of—"

"Damn it all!" Michael grumbled, turning back around from the table.

"You hit my ball, didn't you?"

"Let me guess." Michael blew out a breath. "You want to go second."

Well, that *was* the most strategic way to play; but before Jack could say as much, the little black poodle he'd spotted a while ago ran into the room and lunged itself at Michael's legs.

"Oscar!" his friend laughed, dropping his stick in the process. "How are you, old boy?"

The poodle bounced on his hind legs as though begging Michael to pick him up.

"Know this fellow?" Jack couldn't help but smile.

"My cousin's dog," Michael replied, snatching the little ball of black fluff off the ground and scratching him behind his ears.

"Oh!" Lady Cassandra Priske appeared in the doorway, a slight blush on her cheeks. Tendrils of her dark hair had come out of her chignon as though travel had taken its toll on her usual impeccable appearance, and Jack had never seen a more lovely sight. In fact, seeing her in such disarray made him wonder, not for the first time, what she would look like with her raven locks unbound and spilling over her shoulders to barely cover her breasts from his view. After all, she usually wasn't wearing anything except a smile whenever his imagination took over.

"Lady Cassandra." He bowed slightly. "Such a pleasure to see you." In fact, she was the very reason he'd invited himself along on this unfortunate little journey. She had successfully hidden from him most of last season, but at a secluded castle for the reading of a will…Well, she couldn't hide from him *here*, could she? Not for an extended period of time, anyway.

"Lord St. Giles," she breathed out, her blush deepening.

And the breathy sound to her voice made Jack's cock twitch in response. Yes, following Michael Beck to Keyvnor Castle had been the best idea he'd ever had.

"I didn't know you'd be bringing Oscar," Michael said, drawing Lady Cassandra's attention away from Jack.

"Well, he does make for a more enjoyable traveling companion than Toby."

"That I don't doubt." Michael laughed and then crossed the floor to offer her dog back to her. "Benjamin here with you?"

She shook her head and Jack would have done anything to wrap one of her stray curls around his finger. "Still in Scotland."

"Are you just arriving or are you already settled?"

"Just arrived." She smiled, lighting up the room and lifting Jack's ardor. "And then Oscar ran off. Have you been here long?"

"Charlotte arrived this morning, and Anthony, St. Giles and I arrived yesterday. Already a ton of people here."

Her gaze flicked back to Jack momentarily, though she couldn't quite meet his eyes.

"You haven't—" she glanced down at the dog in her hands "—noticed anything *odd* since you've been here, have you?"

"As in terrifying specters who walk through walls like Grandmother once told us about?" Michael grinned. "No such luck, Cassy. Couldn't even beg the spirits of Keyvnor to assist me in a little game of billiards, unhelpful sods."

She nodded, but still looked slightly uncomfortable.

"Have *you* noticed anything odd?" Jack asked, watching her carefully.

"Man in one of the windows." She shrugged. "He was glaring at me. Probably some distant relative who wants whatever he thinks Papa will inherit, but he did make a chill run down my spine."

Some man was glaring at her? Jack couldn't help but frown. "Well, when you see the fellow again, be sure to point him out to me, Lady Cassandra." The man wouldn't glare at anyone, most especially her, the rest of the time they were in residence.

She finally lifted her warm hazel gaze to meet his, and Jack felt it all the way in his soul. Damn it all, never in his years had any girl ever had such an effect on him. And she had done so ever since he'd first laid eyes on her, so very long ago. One way or the other, he had to do something about it; but she *had* hid from him most of the previous season, at least it seemed like she had. So how exactly could he capture her attention and keep from scaring her away?

CHAPTER 2

"Why in the world is Lord St. Giles here?" Cassy dropped onto a settee across from her cousin Charlotte. Oscar hopped up into the empty space beside her, happily thumping his black tail against the cushions.

"Michael said he invited himself." Charlotte shrugged. "Among others. No idea why they'd want to be here if they didn't have to be."

It was certainly the last place in the world Cassy wanted to be, though the memory of the baron's heated gaze nearly had her fanning herself. She honestly didn't know what to think about St. Giles. He was too charming by half and the most handsome man she'd ever seen with his dark hair and his silvery eyes and that endearing dimple in the middle of his chin, but the way he often watched her was unsettling. Well, it wasn't the way he watched her, not really. It was his *reputation* that was unsettling, which meant she had to be wary with the way he watched her, like she was a sweetmeat he wanted to sample. Of course, if his reputation was to be believed, he'd sampled quite a few sweetmeats in his time. A man like St. Giles was dangerous to any girl who valued her reputation, which Cassy most assuredly did.

She'd successfully thwarted every advance he'd made this last season, but there were so many more people, so many more events, so many places to escape. Castle Keyvnor wasn't small by any stretch of the imagination, but it wasn't so large as the whole of London. It was much easier to evade him and her thoughts of him in Town than it would be here.

A breeze rippled past her and the hair on the back of Cassy's neck stood on end. Oscar barked and stood at attention. "Heavens," she breathed out.

"What's wrong with Oscar?" Charlotte asked.

Cassy blinked at her cousin. "Didn't you feel that?"

Charlotte frowned slightly. "Feel what?"

"Like a breeze or a wind blow through the sitting room?" Gooseflesh crept across her skin.

Charlotte shook her head. "It's an old castle. All the rooms are drafty."

Blast it all. That chill hadn't felt like a draft, but perhaps it was just Cassy's imagination, letting Keyvnor's reputation get the better of her.

Oscar barked again and she glanced down at her dog. He'd noticed the breeze, hadn't he? He'd barked just as it had blown through the room. She wasn't truly mad, or perhaps she was if the only one who was in agreement with her was Oscar.

"Ahem!" Someone cleared her throat in the threshold and Cassy and Charlotte glanced up to find a rather stern looking woman, plump and portly and scowling in their direction. "We do *not* have animals on the furniture at Castle Keyvnor."

"Oh!" Cassy snatched Oscar up in her arms as though to shield him from the scowling woman. He burrowed against her chest.

"Sorry, Mrs. Bray," Charlotte said. "We didn't know."

"Well, now you do." The angry looking woman narrowed her eyes on Cassy.

Heavens, this was an awful place. A sennight. No matter what Papa said, surviving a sennight was going to be nearly impossible.

Charlotte pushed out of her seat and smiled at the woman, which was the last thing in the world Cassy wanted to do. "Um, Mrs. Bray," her cousin began. "I wonder if you could answer a question for me."

"Yes, Lady Charlotte?" She eyed the girl suspiciously.

"Well, I heard tell that there were gypsies on Keyvnor land. Is there any truth to that?"

Gypsies? Castle Keyvnor was becoming less appealing by the moment.

"The Earls of Banfield have always welcomed their lot," Mrs. Bray replied. "They have a camp near Hollybrook Park."

"That is delightful." Charlotte grinned at the news.

Delightful? Charlotte and Cassy had very different ideas as to what constituted delightful.

"You best not be disturbing them." Mrs. Bray warned. "We stay away from them and they stay away from us, even if his lordship welcomed them."

"Yes, of course," Charlotte insisted, briskly nodding her head. "I was simply curious. I would never dream of visiting gypsies."

Cassy sucked in a breath. The last thing in the world she'd ever do was visit a band of gypsies, but she knew her cousin all too well. *Never dream* of visiting gypsies in Charlotte-speak translated into wondering which path was the quickest in reaching them.

The portly woman shrugged and then departed after scowling at Oscar one last time.

With a giant smile, Charlotte dropped back into her seat,

her green eyes shining with glee. "I can't wait to have my fortune told."

"I think you've lost your mind." Cassy shook her head.

Oscar barked in agreement.

Gypsies would probably steal the jewels from Charlotte's hands and tell her something awful for the price.

Her cousin cast her a glance that begged her to keep her tongue on the matter. Then she slid forward in her seat. "It'll be a grand adventure, Cassy, just think a band of marauding gypsies telling tales by the fire. It's just a lark. Something to pass the time while we're here."

"It sounds perfectly horrid."

Charlotte rolled her eyes. "You are too stuffy by half, did you know?"

Cassy frowned in response. "You think *I'm* stuffy? I can't wait to hear you tell Anthony, Harry, and Michael that you mean to visit a band of gypsies." Her brothers, after all, would hardly think the idea a good one.

Instantly, Charlotte's face drained of its color. "You can't tell them!" she insisted. "They'll ruin any bit of enjoyment there is to be had here."

"We're here for the reading of a will, not enjoyment."

"You can find enjoyment anywhere." Her cousin shrugged. "Or at least you can if your overbearing brothers don't know what you're about. You must promise me not to tell them."

"I'm not going to tell them," Cassy promised. Just because she had no desire to seek out gypsies didn't mean she'd betray her cousin's confidence. "But I don't think you should visit them. It could be dangerous and I have an awful feeling about Keyvnor. Don't you feel it too?"

Charlotte shook her head. "I think your imagination is running wild again."

Oscar barked, hopped off Cassy's lap and bolted toward

the doorway where…*Lord St. Giles* was leaned against the doorjamb. At once, Cassy's breath caught in her throat as his gaze heated her anew.

Her poodle sat before the baron and panted up at him as though waiting for a treat. The gentleman winked at her and then lifted a bit of something down to Oscar.

"What did you give him?" Cassy pushed off the settee.

"Charmed a scullery maid for a bit of pheasant."

Why was she not surprised? Was there anyone St. Giles couldn't charm if he put his mind to it? Even Oscar was wagging his tail and looking up at the baron as though he was a knight in shining armor. "Are you attempting to bribe my dog?"

"Bribe? What an ugly word." The grin that spread across his face could have melted her into a puddle if she wasn't already wary of him. "Simply making a new friend. You can never have too many, after all." Then he glanced toward Charlotte. "And your secret is safe with me, my dear. None of your brothers will hear of your expedition into gypsy territory from my lips."

Heavens, how long had he been there? What else had they said that he might have overheard?

"Lord St. Giles," Charlotte breathed out, a red blush staining her cheeks.

The baron stepped further into the sitting room, seeming to take up more space than was his fair share. "I am a firm believer in having a bit of fun every now and then, so I certainly wouldn't stand in the way of you having yours."

"Thank you," her cousin whispered, casting Cassy a sidelong glance.

"Think nothing of it." St. Giles nodded good-naturedly as he rounded the settee, with Oscar following in his wake. Then he stopped just before Cassy. "As for fun, I had hoped we might stroll the gardens, Lady Cassandra."

~

*S*he blinked up at him with those wide hazel eyes of hers and Jack held his breath. The girl had evaded him most of the season. Would she dash his plans now that he'd traveled to godforsaken Cornwall to catch a glimpse of her?

"That might be the most dangerous thing I could do, my lord," she replied.

"You think I'm dangerous?" Jack couldn't help the slow smile that spread across his face. Was that why she'd hidden from him this past spring? That was much preferred to her not liking him. That was surmountable. That he could use to his advantage.

"Well, you certainly have a dangerous reputation." The tiniest amount of pink tinged her cheeks.

Hmm…What had she heard about him? There was no telling. The truth, most likely. So Jack agreed with an incline of his head. "Indeed, though I'm not certain if it will survive should anyone see me with *you*."

Predictably, her mouth fell open. "I beg your pardon?"

What he wouldn't do to taste those lips.

Jack tipped his head in Lady Charlotte's direction. "Even your own cousin finds you stuffy, Lady Cassandra." Then he shrugged. "I'd hate for anyone to think that your stuffiness has rubbed off on *me*. I do have a reputation to protect, after all."

A laugh escaped Lady Charlotte as she said, "I shan't tell a soul."

"Charlotte!" Lady Cassandra blinked at her cousin.

"Well, I'd hate for his reputation to be ruined, besides he is keeping a secret for me."

One never could have too many friends. Jack winked at the lady, silently thanking her for her support. Then he refocused on the one girl who had kept him awake more nights than he could count this past year. He did think she was softening just a bit. Her eyes had that look about them. "If I'm willing to take the chance of walking in the gardens with you, certainly you'll be willing to take the chance of walking with me. I do have more to lose, after all."

She rolled her eyes, but the smile that tipped her lips belied her resistance to him.

"Besides, Oscar will be with us—" he shrugged "—I'm certain if I tried to take any liberties, he'd knock me to the ground to protect your honor."

Lady Cassandra did laugh at that. "He's a little ball of fluff, and after you plied him with pheasant, I'm certain you're his new best friend."

One found friends where and how one could. Honestly, his forward thinking should be rewarded. "Come along, my lady." He offered her his arm. "Just an innocent walk in the gardens. I'll be on my best behavior."

"An innocent walk in the gardens with a dangerous rake?" she asked softly.

"Well, we're the most fun fellows to go for walks with, I can assure you."

CHAPTER 3

*H*eavens. The clouds were dark above Cassy and Lord St. Giles as they stepped into the south gardens, a foreboding grey that stretched across the sky in a most ominous way. She shivered slightly as the same trepidation she'd felt at first seeing Castle Keyvnor washed over her again.

Lord St. Giles patted her fingers that were tucked into the crook of his arm. "Are you all right?"

Was she? Keyvnor was the last place in the world she'd ever want to be, and she might very well have lost her mind to go anywhere with the rakish baron who was far too handsome for his own good, or perhaps for her own good. An intelligent girl should keep her wits about her around a man like him, but a tingle shot through her at his touch anyway. So much for what intelligent girls should do. Cassy tried to shake the sensation away as she gestured to the sky above them. "At the risk of sounding stuffy, walking the gardens doesn't seem the best plan at the moment, my lord."

"Don't tell me you're afraid of a little rain." His brow lifted in question. "What's the worst that could happen?"

Was he serious? "We'll be drenched," she replied. It did look as though a deluge was about to open right above them. Or, she supposed, it was possible ominous clouds always hung above Keyvnor without ever releasing a drop of rain, though that hardly seemed likely. "We'll be soaking wet."

The corner of his mouth tipped upwards, though he seemed to bite back a smile. "Should you become wet, my dear, it'll be my pleasure to take care of you. Happens to be a specialty of mine."

What in the world did *that* mean? Something naughty by the twinkle in his silvery eyes.

Cassy shouldn't encourage him, she really shouldn't. But she couldn't help the laugh that escaped her anyway. "I have a feeling you're even more wicked than I'd first thought."

"Me?" St. Giles blinked at her as though he was completely innocent of the charge. "My dear Lady Cassandra, I feel you've misjudged me."

That she highly doubted. "Have I?"

"Mmm." He agreed with a nod of his head. "A stroll through the gardens hardly sounds wicked." Then he dropped his voice a bit. "Though I could always suggest we lose ourselves in the hedge maze for an hour or so, if we feel like being the tiniest bit wicked."

She spotted the maze off in the distance and an uneasiness that had nothing to do with the rakish baron's suggestion rippled through her. The idea of being *lost* anywhere at Keyvnor was enough to make her skin crawl, but the maze in particular seemed rather menacing. Cassy shook her head. "I'd rather not be lost anywhere here."

A slightly perplexed look flashed in his eyes but then he smiled, which did send a thrill through her. Foolish girl that she was. "Whatever you desire, my lady."

He squeezed her fingers once more and led her down a path with a hedge on one side and lovely Cornish daisies and some purplish-blue flowers she wasn't familiar with on the other. Panting, Oscar happily followed in their wake.

"What *are* you doing at Castle Keyvnor?" Cassy cast him a sidelong glance. It didn't, after all, make any sense that he'd be there for the reading of her late-great-uncle's will.

"Walking the gardens with the loveliest girl in all of England," he replied evenly, though he didn't take his eyes from the path.

Cassy's cheeks warmed a bit at the compliment. Still, that wasn't what she meant, and he well knew it. "Are you a distant relation of Banfield's of some sort?"

Lord St. Giles shook his head. "Just thought to keep Michael company. We were enjoying ourselves at Newmarket when he got the summons."

"So you're just being a good friend?" she asked, not quite believing that at all.

"Are you suggesting otherwise, my dear?" he returned smoothly.

Before she could reply to that, Oscar barked behind them. Cassy slid her hand from the baron's arm and spun around. Her dog barked again, focused on a spot in the nearby daisies like there was something hiding amongst the plethora of white flowers.

Lord St. Giles' hand settled at the small of her back, startling her with his familiarity, yet it was soothing at the same time. "Does he often do that? Bark for no reason?"

No, he never did. Cassy shook her head. "Perhaps there *is* something there."

"Something in the flowers we can't see?"

She glanced away from Oscar to find Lord St. Giles' gaze firmly focused on her. "Perhaps."

His brow lifted in question.

Blast it all. He was going to think she was ridiculous, just like her family did. Cassy heaved a sigh. "This place doesn't feel right to me. I can't put my finger on it, but I sensed it as we arrived. Have you truly noticed nothing?"

A crease marred Lord St. Giles's handsome brow. "Is this because of the fellow who was scowling at you?"

Cassy supposed the angry man in black did have something to do with her uneasiness, though she'd been uneasy about this visit ever since Papa had been summoned to attend the late earl's will reading. "The idea of Keyvnor has always made me uncomfortable and being here in person has only made me more so."

And then a loud roar sounded directly behind them.

Cassy stumbled backwards and would have fallen to the ground if Lord St. Giles hadn't grasped her waist and kept her upright. Before she could even let out a wail, the sound of Toby's familiar cackling reached her ears.

"Did you think Great-uncle Banfield was here to murder you, Cassy?" her rotten little brother howled with glee.

"Heavens, Toby!" she breathed out. "You took five years off my life!"

~

*J*ack made certain Lady Cassandra was steady on her feet before he turned his full attention on the troublesome lad who seemed quite pleased with himself. "Friend of yours?" he muttered to the lady at his side.

"My brother is the furthest thing from my friend," she grumbled.

Something Jack's older sisters might very well have said about him more than once over the years. "St. Giles," he said to the lad. "And you are?"

The gleeful little bastard tipped his head back regally. "Toby Priske."

"Well, Toby, I believe you owe your sister an apology."

The boy's dark eyes sparkled with something akin to mischief and he shrugged. "Since I'm not sorry…"

Lady Cassandra breathed out a sigh. "You're wasting your breath, my lord. Toby only ever apologizes when Papa forces him to do so." Then she glared at her younger brother. "I believe his last threat was to have you drawn and quartered. I shouldn't wish to be you when he finds out about this."

The boy shrugged again. "He said if I annoyed you again in the *coach*. We're not in the coach any longer."

Normally, domestic squabbles wouldn't be something Jack would trouble himself with; however, if he was honest, he'd once tormented his sisters in much the same fashion as Toby Priske was doing now. If he should find a way to curtail the lad's plans, or perhaps redirect him in a more useful way, he might just gain Lady Cassandra's favor. And having her favor was something Jack would be quite glad to have.

To that end, he laughed. "You do remind me of myself, Toby."

Lady Cassandra cast him a sidelong frown. She'd forgive him in a minute. He'd make certain of it.

"I was plagued with three older sisters." Jack shook his head. "*Three*. Can you imagine all the squabbles over ribbons and dresses and other such inanities?"

"Sisters are the worst," the boy agreed, seeming quite pleased to have Jack on his side.

"They are, indeed." Jack nodded. "Unfortunately, my backside was forever sore as my humorless father never saw the genius in any of my schemes. At least until…"

Toby Priske leaned a little closer. The whole thing was almost too easy. "Until…" he prodded.

"Well, until I learned one little detail that got my schemes rewarded instead of punished."

Lady Cassandra watched him just as closely as her

brother was, but Jack forced himself not to smile lest he give his current scheme away.

"What did you learn?" the boy asked.

Jack glanced around the gardens as though he was making sure they couldn't be overheard. "You may not believe me, but on my word it's the truth." He tipped his head toward the beautiful brunette who'd drifted in and out of his thoughts for more than a year. "Your sister is quite breathtaking."

The boy gagged, and Jack managed not to laugh. Had anyone told him that about any of his sisters when he was Toby's age, he might very well have become ill himself.

"Believe me, I felt the same about my sisters." Jack gestured to Lady Cassandra. "But look at her. Now I don't expect you to see the girl *I* see. But take my word for it. Your sister has beautiful dark hair some fellow would love to caress. The prettiest eyes some men would fight each other to drown in. And the softest lips more than a few duplicitous rakes would love to kiss. Simply put, your sister is beyond beautiful."

Lady Cassandra's cheeks turned a very pretty pink, though Jack continued to focus his attention on her younger brother.

"I don't see any of that." The boy turned up his nose at the picture Jack was painting.

"I certainly never saw it with my sisters either," Jack agreed. "And yet, it's the truth. And as her brother, it is your duty to make certain black-hearted scoundrels keep their distance from her. Did you realize that?"

"There aren't any scoundrels who want *her*." Toby shook his head in disbelief.

Jack couldn't resist winking at Lady Cassandra as he said, "Oh, I can assure you there's at least one." Then he refocused his attention on her brother. "Instead of pestering her, you should be devising ways to thwart the plots of scurrilous blackguards who have her in their sights."

"Thwart their plots?" the lad echoed, his brow scrunched up a bit.

"Of course." Jack nodded. "I can't image your parents would ever get angry with you for keeping your sisters *safe*. I know my father was quite pleased with my efforts to do so." He grinned at the boy. "Suddenly all of my plans were rewarded once they were focused on my sisters' suitors, not that *they* ever thanked me for my troubles on their behalf; but sisters, as you know, are an ungrateful lot."

"Mmm." The boy nodded in agreement. "So you plotted against their suitors?"

And just that easily, Jack had redirected the boy away from making trouble for Lady Cassandra. And should he happen to scare off any of her other suitors in the process, all the better for Jack. "This one time," he confided, "I splashed some ink into the tea of one of the fellows who was chasing after my oldest sister. Completely blackened the man's teeth and he wasn't seen in public for sennight."

Toby cackled. "That's brilliant!"

"My lord!" Lady Cassandra touched a hand to her heart in apparent mortification.

But Jack only grinned at her brother, his new partner in crime. After all, if he was suddenly the boy's confidant and helped supply him with ideas to thwart *other* fellows, Toby Priske wouldn't use those same plots against Jack, and if he tried, Jack would see it coming from a mile away. "I have hundreds of ideas," he told him. "And I'll be happy to share them with you if you notice some *other* fellow chasing after her skirts. I'm sure your father will thank you for your efforts."

"You're too kind to help my brother, my lord," Lady Cassandra narrowed her eyes on him.

"Well—" Jack shrugged "—we younger brothers have to stick together."

Her brother preened at that; and unless Jack was mistaken, there was a little glint in her eyes as though she'd just sorted him out.

"You'll let me know if you notice anyone hanging on her every word? Or paying her too much attention, won't you?" he continued.

"Of course," the boy agreed. "And you'll give me ideas to help me dispense with them?"

"It would be my pleasure," Jack assured him. "But as *I* am keeping watch over the lady now, you can safely run along and enjoy your time at Keyvnor. No need to worry about her when she's with me."

Toby nodded. "I'd best go see if there are any inkpots in the study." And then he took off at a sprint.

"My father will not thank you for that," she said at his side.

Jack shrugged. "It'll keep him from tormenting you."

"And hurt my chances with some decent fellow."

At that Jack laughed. "My dear, what would you want with some decent fellow, when you have me?"

She seemed to bite back a smile, which Jack took as a great victory. "Are you never serious, my lord?"

He tucked her hand back into the crook of his arm again. "Only when it's absolutely required."

"And when is that?"

"Usually when dealing with my father. Or whenever I'm picking out the right jacket to catch my eyes," he teased. "Did this blue do the trick?" Then he dipped his head down so she could directly meet his gaze.

She shook her head, though her hazel eyes were twinkling just like he'd hoped. "You are mad."

Jack winked at her. "I've been called worse." He leaned in

27

to press his lips to hers, but before he could kiss her, a large raindrop landed on her nose.

She released his arm and leapt backwards in surprise. "Oh!" she squealed.

And then thunder rolled overhead.

"Come on, Oscar!" Lady Cassandra lifted the edge of her skirts and started back toward the castle.

Jack blew out a breath as he watched the lady and her little black poodle rush back for the safety of Keyvnor's shelter. Damn it all! He'd been so bloody close to tasting those lips.

CHAPTER 4

*C*assy sighed as she dropped onto the edge of her borrowed four-poster. St. Giles had called her *breathtaking,* and…She leaned back against her pillows and closed her eyes, wanting to remember the rest just as he'd said it. He wanted to caress her hair and drown in her eyes and kiss her lips. She sighed again as she thought about how close he'd come to doing that last one. What would it be like to kiss him?

A wet nose brushed against her cheek and she couldn't help but laugh. "Oscar!" She opened her eyes and patted the top of her poodle's head. "I know what doggy kisses are like."

Though she still had no idea what it was like to kiss a rogue or…Well, he'd called himself a scoundrel, hadn't he? A *scoundrel.* He made the word sound so appealing the way he said it. St. Giles was such a mix between charm and danger, and… Oh, if only it hadn't started raining and he *had* kissed her. At least she'd know what it was like instead wondering about it.

Cassy was being foolish, of course. Dashing as the scoundrel was, the last thing she should even think about doing was kissing him. He *did* have a certain reputation, after all.

Oscar dropped down onto the bed beside her and Cassy smiled at her poodle. He was such a sweet boy. "We'll both be in for it if that awful Mrs. Bray finds out you're on the bed." But the fact of the matter was Oscar slept on Cassy's bed every night back home at Widcombe Hall, and she had no intention of making her beloved little dog sleep on the floor at Keyvnor, horrid place that—

A dark shadow darted across the room! She spotted it out of the corner of her eye, but it was definitely there.

Oh, good heavens! Cassy bolted upright and screamed as the shapeless mass dissolved into the ether right before her eyes. She screamed again as she scrambled off the bed. There was no way she was staying here. Not one night.

Cassy threw open her door and rushed into the corridor, barreling right into her father. She'd never been so happy to see him.

"Good God, Cassandra," Papa breathed out, looking at her as though she'd lost her mind. "What's the matter with you?"

Heavens! Cassy's heart was racing and she couldn't quite catch her voice.

Beside her, Oscar barked as though he was explaining the situation to her father. Papa, however, didn't speak dog. He narrowed his eyes on Cassy. "Was that you screaming just now?"

She nodded quickly and managed to find her voice. "There was a shadow in my room, Papa."

"A shadow?" A muscle ticked in his jaw. "Cassandra Eloise Priske, you will *not* start this ghost nonsense, do you understand me?"

Perfect. Papa was in a mood. But she *had* seen something. If only he'd listen. "There *was* a shadow, Papa. Oscar saw it too. And a chill in the drawing room. And something in the gardens."

His face began to turn red. "Not. One. More. Word."

But there were so many other words she wanted to say. She wanted to tell him that she wasn't imaging these things. She wanted to tell him how hurt she was that he didn't believe her. And she wanted to tell him that she'd gladly walk all the way back home to Somerset instead of spending one night at Keyvnor. But the angry expression on her father's face did not bode well for her if she so much as sighed her displeasure.

"Dinner will be served at the top of the hour," Papa continued. "Don't make others wait on you."

Heavens! He'd had to wait for her one time. *One time* in her nineteen years. One would think that a single event such as that would have long been forgotten by now. It apparently wasn't, however, so Cassy nodded instead of speaking.

~

"*D*o try to keep from catching my father's notice," Michael whispered to Jack as the Marquess of Halesworth entered the great room and glanced in their direction.

"Your father doesn't care for me?" That was news. Jack had always assumed the marquess liked him. At least it always seemed as though Halesworth thought well of him.

"He doesn't care for the fact that I brought friends to a will reading," Michael muttered under his breath. "Already read me the riot act which Anthony, the stuffed up prig, found vastly amusing."

That did sound like something Michael's oldest brother would enjoy. He glanced around the great room and nodded toward his friend's second brother who'd just returned from a long stint in the navy. "And what about Lord Harry?" The man had been at sea most of the time Jack had been acquainted with Michael and he didn't have any sort of grasp on the fellow at all.

"Pompous prig," Michael returned. "Sat there the whole time Father was dressing me down and barely blinked his eyes. He and Anthony are cut from the same wearisome cloth."

"In that case," Jack said, "it's probably a very good thing you did bring me along, then."

Michael chuckled at that. "Just as long as you don't do anything that will draw Father's ire while we're here."

Jack shook his head. Halesworth he could handle, at least he thought he could. Handling Lord Widcombe was another matter, indeed. Lady Cassandra's father seemed much more forbidding than her uncle did. Rigid and humorless. He'd probably get along famously with Jack's father, honestly, complaining about the weather and their ungrateful children. That was the problem, however. If Jack hadn't, in his twenty-six years on Earth, figured out how to manage his father, how was he going to manage Lady Cassandra's?

And speaking of the lady, where was Cassandra? Shouldn't she be gathering with everyone else to head into dinner? How could he manage to secure a spot beside her if she didn't show up soon?

"St. Giles!" Toby Priske bounded into the great room with a giant smile.

Though he wasn't the Priske Jack wanted to see, he smiled at the boy anyway. "Toby." He nodded in greeting.

The lad rushed toward Jack and Michael. "I searched the study over and I *did* find two jars of ink."

"Two jars of ink?" Michael echoed.

Toby nodded quickly. "In case I have to dump them into anyone's tea while we're here."

"Why the devil would you dump ink into anyone's tea?" The horrified expression that splashed onto Michael's face was vastly amusing, and it took quite a bit of effort for Jack not to laugh.

The young boy looked from his cousin to Jack and back again. "St. Giles said I needed to keep an eye out for any scoundrels chasing after Cassy's and Sam's skirts and I should dump ink in their tea."

"Well, that's not exactly what I said," Jack began, but his friend cut him off.

"Have you lost your mind? That's exactly the sort of thing that will draw my father's ire."

Jack shrugged slightly. "You and your brothers keep a watchful eye on Lady Charlotte. I simply suggested that Toby should keep a watchful eye on his sisters and to not let any blackguards get too close to them."

"And he should do that by dumping ink in some fellow's tea?" Michael's brow lifted in question.

"Not that precisely," Jack continued. "I just told Toby how I had done that very thing years ago to one of Helen's suitors. I didn't suggest he toss ink willy-nilly into just anyone's tea."

Michael released a pent-up sigh. "Toby, do *not* dump ink into anyone's *anything*, not while we're at Keyvnor, in any event."

The lad frowned up at his cousin with confusion.

Then Michael glared at Jack. "And don't give him any more ideas while we're here."

Lady Cassandra stepped into the great room, at that moment, her arm linked with her sister's. Jack's voice caught in his throat at the sight of the lady. Her dark hair was piled high on her head with ringlets framing her face, and the bodice of her pink gown was low enough to make his mouth water.

Jack cleared his throat. "I'll be happy to keep an eye on

your sisters, Toby, while we're here. You can start plotting ways to keep their suitors at bay for when you're back in Somerset or in London."

Jack ignored the incredulous expression on Michael's face. How could he be expected to focus on anything other than Lady Cassandra when she met his gaze and the sweetest little smile graced her lips?

"And perhaps we should forget about tossing ink into anything," Michael muttered.

But Toby shook his head. "St. Giles said some fellows want to caress Cassy's hair and kiss her." He made a face like me might be ill. "I'd better be on the look out."

Michael sent Jack a sidelong glance. "*Some fellows* better watch themselves while we're here."

"Toby!" Lord Widcombe called from across the room. "You should be having supper in the nursery with the other children."

The boy's shoulders sagged a bit. "I'm not a baby, Father."

"Nor are you an adult," Widcombe returned. "Nursery. Now."

Toby glanced up at Jack and Michael as he started from the great room. "I'll keep thinking up ideas, St. Giles."

Before Jack could even respond to the departing boy, Michael jabbed him in his side with his elbow. "Are you chasing after Cassy's skirts?"

Only since the moment Jack had first spotted her. Michael would have realized that long before now if he hadn't been focused on the stream of skirts he'd been chasing instead. Even so, Jack wasn't about to admit as much to his friend. The man, after all, was fairly overprotective of his own sister, and Michael knew Jack better than most. Odds were, that overprotective instinct might also apply to his cousin and Jack would rather not risk that. "Don't you think she's a tad innocent for me?" he hedged.

Michael snorted. "I think she's *a lot* innocent for you. Though I'm not sure that's ever stopped you before."

"I promise not to do anything to catch your father's notice."

"I do not feel reassured," Michael complained as Jack started in the direction of the beautiful Priske sisters. It was the brunette, however, who had his full attention.

⁓

"Shadows are everywhere," Samantha said reasonably. "They move and change shape with light all the time."

"They don't move like this one did," Cassy returned under her breath as the dashing Lord St. Giles started in her direction, and her heart increased its beat. "And they don't disappear into thin air either."

Her sister scoffed. "Please don't say that to Papa."

Cassy already had, not that it had done one bit of good, but before she could say as much, St. Giles was right before them. "My lady, we meet again," he said as he lifted her fingers to his lips.

Cassy's breath hitched and she was certain her heart might beat right out of her chest. "My lord."

"Tell me," he began, "do you see the fellow who scowled at you earlier? I would like a word with him."

Cassy glanced out at the sea of people gathered in the great room. The place was teeming with relations, honestly. Her aunt and uncle. Her cousins. Distant relatives, a number of fellows she'd seen in society, and even more that she'd never seen before. But none of them were the angry looking man she'd spotted from the window earlier in the day. "I don't see him." And if the fellow wasn't with the assembled masses, who was he? A servant?

Lord St. Giles sighed slightly. "If you do spot him, I'd like to know it."

She nodded, feeling the tiniest bit relieved that he seemed so genuinely concerned about her.

"I had hoped you'd allow me to escort you to dinner." And though his words were innocent enough, his eyes focused on her lips and Cassy's cheeks heated from his attention.

"Don't talk about ghosts," Samantha whispered.

St. Giles heard her, however. An amused sparkle lit his eyes. "Lady Cassandra, don't tell me you believe there's any merit to the tales of Keyvnor's hauntings."

Blast it all. She liked it much more when he was flirting with her than mocking her. "I believe there's something else here. I can feel it." Even if she did sound like a Bedlamite in admitting so.

"My dear," he began, sounding slightly patronizing. "You sound like Michael. I doubt there is one square inch in all of Britain where someone hasn't died at some point in history. If something like ghosts were truly real, don't you think they'd be everywhere? That there would be some evidence of them all around us all the time?"

"You sound very logical, my lord," she countered. "And yet, something has made me uneasy ever since I arrived. And something terrified my grandmother when she lived here." Cassy breathed out a sigh of relief when she spotted her cousin Anthony across the room. *He* wouldn't diminish her fears, and he would probably keep St. Giles at bay. "Do excuse me. I believe I'll allow Redgrave to escort me into dinner this evening."

CHAPTER 5

*I*rritating as it was, Jack had to admit he'd played that whole thing foolishly. He very rarely did that; and the fact that he'd done so with Cassandra Priske was more than frustrating. Instead of enjoying her company over dinner, he'd had to watch from another table as she conversed with her overly serious cousin all evening while he found himself between the Marchioness of Halesworth and one of the new Earl of Banfield's daughters. He wasn't certain which one she was, and he didn't particularly care. He did, however, care a great deal that Lady Cassandra hadn't looked even once in his direction during dinner. Damn it all.

If he could just take back those last few words he'd said to her. Who would have known she was so sensitive about the whole subject of ghosts? She seemed like such a reasonable, levelheaded girl, honestly. The fact that she very clearly believed in such things should give him pause, but it didn't. He just needed to find a way to remedy his misstep and get back into her good graces.

It was a relief when dinner came to an end and the ladies excused themselves. All Jack had to do was find a way to avoid port with the gentlemen and go in search of Lady Cassandra to smooth the feathers he'd ruffled.

To that end, he pushed out of his chair, prepared to make his excuses when Anthony Beck, Viscount Redgrave, clapped a hand to his shoulder and pushed Jack back into his seat. Bloody perfect. Redgrave was hardly a jolly fellow on his best day and the man *had* spent all of dinner talking to his cousin Cassandra. A very stiff warning was about to be leveled on Jack, not that he hadn't experienced his fair share of stiff warnings in the past, but...Well, any time he spent in Redgrave's company was time that would be better spent in reclaiming his lost ground with the man's cousin. "Now—" he began.

But Redgrave cut him off, "I'm headed over to Hollybrook Park tomorrow."

Hollybrook Park? That did sound familiar. "Oh?" Jack eyed the viscount, trying to sort out the man's game.

"Thomas Vail's funeral services. I thought you might want to join me."

Damn it all. Jack released the breath he was holding. Now that he thought about it, the Vails *did* live in Hollybrook Park. That's why the place sounded familiar. But funeral services? "Thomas Vail has died?"

Redgrave nodded. "Received a missive from Adam Vail upon my arrival. Thought the fellow could use a friendly face or two."

Thomas Vail was dead? Jack hadn't thought about the lothario in a million years. Once upon a time, he'd been a right jolly fellow who'd cut his swath through London, at least until he'd become too ill to do so any longer. Jack had almost completely forgotten about the man. Out of sight, out of mind and all that. Still, he had gone to school with Adam Vail. They weren't the best of friends, but he'd liked the man well enough. "Haven't seen him in years."

Redgrave shrugged. "No one has. Came back to Cornwall when his brother took ill."

And stayed? In Godforsaken Cornwall? Jack would have gone stark raving mad. "Well, of course, I'll be happy to attend the services with you."

Redgrave narrowed his eyes slightly on Jack and said, "And in the meantime, you can steer clear of Cassandra Priske."

Damn it all. Redgrave had sidetracked him with the whole Thomas Vail funeral service thing. "Shouldn't you be focusing your concern on Lady Charlotte instead? She *is* your sister, after all."

"True." The viscount raked his eyes across Jack. "Benjamin Priske should be the one keeping an eye on Cassandra, but since he's in Scotland..."

Since Priske was in Scotland, Redgrave would take over for his cousin in dolling out warnings to scoundrels and rakes alike. "The lady has nothing to worry about from me."

Redgrave didn't look convinced. He heaved a sigh. "Yes, well, see that she doesn't."

With Redgrave at his side, it was impossible for Jack to make his escape, and he had to suffer through port until the gentlemen decided to rejoin the ladies.

As soon as he stepped into the great room, he scanned the place, looking for his quarry, but Lady Cassandra was nowhere to be found. Damn it all. He felt Redgrave's eyes on him, but Jack made his way to Lady Charlotte's side anyway.

She smiled up at him in greeting. "My lord."

Jack tipped his head toward her oldest brother. "I do hope you were able to have a bit of fun this afternoon, Lady

Charlotte, and that certain prison wardens didn't thwart your plans."

Her grin widened. "Indeed I made it all the way to the gypsy camp without any of my brothers being the wiser."

"I am glad to hear it." Jack grinned in return. "From one secret keeper to another, would you mind terribly pointing me in the direction of Lady Cassandra?"

At that, Lady Charlotte's brow scrunched up a bit. "Cassy said she wasn't feeling well and retired early, my lord."

"Just my luck." Jack blew out a breath.

"Better luck tomorrow."

Hoping his luck would change was a damned frustrating place to be. "Thank you, my dear. And best of luck in thwarting your wardens the rest of the week."

~

*C*assy stepped over the threshold of her borrowed chambers. She couldn't help but search the place over with her gaze, looking for any evidence of that black shadow she'd seen earlier. But there was nothing, nothing out of the ordinary anywhere. The antique armoire in the corner looked rather charming against the flickering candlelight and the walls did seem as though they'd been freshly scrubbed. There wasn't a cobweb or stray shadow anywhere in sight, and Oscar was sleeping quite soundly in the middle of her four-poster.

Perhaps she had imagined that shadow earlier. Perhaps she *had* let the tales of Keyvnor get the best of her and turn her into a blathering ninny. Certainly, Lord St. Giles thought so. Not that Cassy should let anything St. Giles thought mean anything to her one way or another. He was devastatingly handsome. He was too charming for his own good. And just being near him made her heart pound and her breath catch. But, the truth was, he was also rather dangerous and she shouldn't let his opinion on anything sway her in one direction or another. Even if he was very possibly right about the number of people who had died in any one place throughout the history of the world. If they were all ghosts...

A scratch came at her door and Cassy let out a yelp as her heart leapt to her throat.

Oscar woke up and barked at the sound.

Heavens, she was a ninny! Cassy placed her hand over her heart to help calm its pounding and called, "Yes?"

"Lady Cassandra." Betsy, her maid, pushed the door open and looked at her as though she was a foreign species. "Are you ready to undress for the evening?"

A staggered breath escaped Cassy. Was she ready to sleep at Castle Keyvnor? Her pulse began to pound at just the thought. But she was being foolish again. "Yes," she said softly. "I believe I am ready to turn in for the night."

Betsy glanced toward Oscar and frowned slightly. "Mrs. Bray was quite stern with me about Oscar being on the furniture."

Well, Mrs. Bray could take a flying leap from Keyvnor's tallest turret. "What Mrs. Bray doesn't know won't kill her," Cassy returned. Besides, Oscar slept with her every night at Widcombe Hall, and he'd never once caused any sort of damage.

"Yes, of course, milady," Betsy replied, looking uneasy.

"What's wrong?" Cassy asked, stepping closer to her maid.

But Betsy simply shook her head. "Mrs. Bray just doesn't seem like the warmest woman and I'd rather not get on her bad side."

"I met her myself today, Betsy, and I'm not certain if Mrs. Bray has a good side."

Her maid did laugh at that as she crossed behind Cassy. "No, I'm not certain she does either." She began working the fastenings of Cassy's gown. "I'd never tell a soul about Oscar, I just wanted to warn you."

"Have you spoken to many members of Keyvnor's staff today?"

Cassy's dress sagged at her bodice as Betsy made quick work of the fastenings and then the muslin pooled at her feet. "A few," she replied in a way that sounded as though she was holding her tongue about something.

"And?" Cassy glanced back over her shoulder at the girl.

"And—" Betsy looked sheepish "—Mrs. Bray may be the nicest of the bunch."

Heavens! If that was true, the staff at Keyvnor could probably scare away any ghosts who'd taken up residence in the castle. "A sennight," she echoed her father's earlier words. "We only have to survive a sennight, Betsy."

"Aye, milady."

After dressing for bed and dismissing her maid, Cassy and Oscar snuggled under the counterpane. Candlelight flickered against walls, but Cassy had no intention of blowing out the light. How was she to see about the room in the darkness? How was she to make certain there was nothing ghostly to be seen without the light for assistance?

Oscar burrowed against her and Cassy kissed the top of his little head. "Very glad you're here, my sweet boy."

Her poodle sighed as though he was quite content to be with her too and she couldn't help but smile.

Cassy watched the flickering light against the walls even as her eyelids grew heavy, and then she couldn't keep them open any longer. Sleep took her quickly and deeply somewhere far away where a handsome man with an endearing dimple in his chin didn't think she was foolish and had her wrapped in his arms and…

42

A bone-chilling scream from somewhere in the castle jolted her awake in the middle of the night.

What in the world was *that*? Cassy sat bolt upright as Oscar barked. She clutched her poodle to her, struggled to catch her breath, and scanned her chambers once more. Heavens! She might never survive this sennight!

CHAPTER 6

*S*obering. There wasn't another word to accurately describe Thomas Vail's funeral service other than sobering…Well, *odd*. Jack supposed the whole thing had been rather odd as well. Until that morning, he hadn't realized how very little he'd actually known the Vail brothers. For one thing, he had no idea they were half gypsies. He wasn't certain how he'd missed that fact over the years, and seeing Adam sporting red at the service and an unshaved beard had been…Well, *odd*, for lack of a better word. Jack couldn't imagine showing up at anyone's funeral dressed the way Adam Vail had been that morning. If he did so, he was fairly certain his own father would keel over dead from the shock…Which, now that Jack thought about it, might be worth the experiment.

Still, it was difficult to believe Thomas Vail had died, and to learn the cause of his death was unnerving. *The pox?* It hardly even seemed possible that so virile a man should die from that very virility. The merest mention of the word had made Jack shift uncomfortably in his seat. Damn it all, suffering from the pox was a fate worse than death, and

Thomas was quite fortunate to have been released from that hellish existence. The whole thing made the idea of monogamy worth a serious look. Well, monogamy with the right lady, of course.

As if on cue, the right lady strolled into the parlor, looking quite distraught. Her poodle took one look at Jack, wagged his tail and bolted across the room to sit at Jack's feet.

Jack pushed out of his seat at Lady Cassandra's entrance and his heart twisted at the sight of dark circles around her eyes and the unnatural paleness of her skin. "My lady." He stepped around Oscar. "Are you all right?"

A tight smile settled on her lips. "Nothing a return to Widcombe Hall won't solve."

So she hadn't slept well. The circles around her eyes said as much. Poor girl. She did hate being at Keyvnor. Jack offered her his arm and a smile. "Difficult time sleeping last night?"

She shrugged and made no attempt to accept his offered arm. "Oscar went missing this morning and I couldn't find him."

He glanced down at the poodle who'd since followed him across the room. Alas, he didn't have a bit of pheasant to offer the little dog today. "I'm glad he returned himself to you."

"He never runs off at home. It's almost as though he can't help himself at Keyvnor."

Jack nodded. "A new place with new smells and new things to investigate. You can hardly blame the little fellow."

"I suppose so." Lady Cassandra blew out a breath and she looked even more uncomfortable all of a sudden.

"What is it, my lady?"

Her brow squished up and she shook her head. "Never mind."

Oh, damn it all. He was farther from earning her trust now than he had been yesterday. "Please tell me. Perhaps I can be of assistance."

She pursed her very kissable lips and then asked, "Did *you* hear a scream in the middle of the night?"

Jack had slept like the dead, which was probably not the best turn of phrase considering the way their conversation had gone the previous evening. So he simply shook his head. "*You* heard someone scream?"

She glanced at his still proffered arm and then into his eyes, a wariness in hers. "Not that I expect you to believe me."

Well, now was the perfect time for Jack to make his apologies. "I have no reason to doubt you, Lady Cassandra. I do hope I haven't made it seem as though I ever would." He glanced down at his arm once more, still waiting for her to take it. He was starting to look like a fool.

"My father doesn't believe me." When her hand slid around his elbow, Jack felt as though he'd won a small victory and he breathed a sigh of relief.

"My dear, I do hope you won't ever confuse me with your father."

A small laugh escaped Lady Cassandra and her warm hazel eyes brightened a little. "Is there anyone you can't charm, my lord?"

He didn't particularly care if he charmed anyone else for the rest of his life, not as long as he was always able to charm her. "My own father," he answered truthfully and gestured toward the large window. "Shall we make another attempt to stroll the gardens this afternoon, my lady?"

She hesitated before answering. "With all the rain this morning? I'm certain I'd sink down to my knees."

That might be true, but Jack wasn't ready to relinquish her company. So perhaps another tactic. "What about billiards, then? Have you ever played?"

She looked at him as though he'd lost his mind. "Billiards?"

It was an unconventional suggestion, but Jack had never been known for being orthodox. "I'm happy to teach you," he replied, and he would be only too happy to stand behind her, grasp her waist in his hands and whisper instructions in her ear. Just the idea of it, would make him hard as a fire iron. He could just imagine her leaning over the billiard table, her bottom sticking out over the edge, and it was all he could do not to groan.

"I'm sure my father wouldn't approve of that."

"Then let's not tell him." Jack winked at her. "Our little secret."

Lady Cassandra's pale cheeks flushed pink. "And once I leave Keyvnor, who would I ever play with, then?"

"I'm certain I could make arrangements to play with you as often as you'd like."

A slight smile tipped her lips. "Are you saying you'd visit me in Somerset?"

He was fairly certain he'd travel to the ends of the Earth to visit her. Traveling to Somerset would hardly be an inconvenience. "Would you like for me to?"

∽

*C*assy's cheeks stung. There was no question she was in over her head with Lord St. Giles. He was so much more practiced in the art of flirtation. The look in his eyes, as though she was the prettiest girl in the world, nearly took her breath away.

She cleared her throat. "I would think that your doing so would affect your dangerous reputation, should anyone learn you were visiting stuffy old me, my lord. And I know how much you value that reputation of yours."

He tipped back his head and laughed. "I should have known my own words would get used against me at some point."

Cassy couldn't help but smile in return. Lord St. Giles's laugh was so warm and genuine. And after the night she'd suffered through, just being in his presence did make her feel the tiniest bit safer.

"But I would gladly toss my dangerous reputation away —" he seemed to sober a bit "—if I could persuade you to play a little billiards with me."

Heavens. Papa would have an apoplexy if he found out she was participating in such a masculine sport. Still, Papa hadn't listened to her about any of her fears, so why was she overly concerned about what *he* would think? "You promise not to tell anyone?" she asked. After all, it was one thing to worry about whether or not Papa found out about her playing billiards and quite another for society as a whole to know she engaged in such a game with Lord St. Giles.

"You have my word," he vowed.

And though he was known as a bit of a scoundrel and she wasn't quite certain what his word was worth, Cassy did find solace in that vow. "Do you think you could teach me to play well enough that I could beat Michael?"

St. Giles laughed again. "That shall take less than one afternoon, my dear."

In no time, Cassy found herself in the billiard room along with the devilish baron, staring at the table before them, testing the weight of a cue stick in her hand while Oscar sat guard at the door.

St. Giles placed a white ball near one end of the table. "The first shot is called the lag," he began. "You can often beat Michael at this stage of the game."

Cassy laughed. "There's only one ball on the table."

The baron seemed to bite back a grin. "Sometimes, my

dear, that is all it takes." He gestured to the table once more. "With your stick, you line up your shot and hit the ball so it will bounce off the far end of the table and roll back toward you. The player whose ball comes the closest to the cushion on this side of the table without hitting it wins the lag."

"And what if you hit the cushion?" she asked, trying to figure out how one could make the ball stop in the right place.

"Then you'll forfeit the lag."

"What if both people hit the cushion?"

He laughed. "Both people won't hit the cushion, Cassandra."

A tingle coursed through her at the familiar way with which he addressed her. She shook her head to refocus on the matter at hand. "But what if they did?"

"Then neither of them should be playing billiards," he returned with a grin. "Now if *you* win the lag, do you suppose you want to go first or second?"

It generally was best to go first in all games, wasn't it? "First?" she guessed.

But St. Giles shook his head, and his dark hair fell across his brow. "After the lag, we'll set up the table." He brushed his hair from his face. "The player who goes first is always at a disadvantage because they're breaking the balls apart. The fellow, or *lady*, who goes second has the advantage of setting up their shot with a more open table."

"All right." Cassy supposed that made sense, more sense than figuring out how to get the lag ball to stop in the right place.

"Now—" he gestured to the white ball on the table "—come over here and set up your shot."

Cassy made her way to the small side of the table where St. Giles was standing. She'd seen Benjamin and her cousins play before, so she knew she was supposed to lean over the table and hit the white ball with the tip of her stick, but it seemed a little unruly. "I just move it like this?" she asked, jabbing the stick toward the ball.

She probably looked like a fool, and she certainly felt like one; but he didn't laugh. In fact, his silvery eyes sparkled with something that looked like adoration. "With just a bit more finesse." He stepped behind her and settled his hand on her waist.

The heat of his touch nearly seared her through the muslin of her gown and she couldn't quite breathe.

And then the baron was pressed up against her back and said very softly in her ear, "You want your cue to land right in the middle of the ball and to send it straight across the table. If you tap it on one side or the other, you'll never get it to bounce off the far cushion properly."

The very last things in the world Cassy could concentrate on was the far cushion or the little white ball, not with him so close to her, not with his touch robbing her of her breath, not with the heat of his breath against her neck and the sandalwood scent of him swirling around her.

"Cassandra," he rumbled her name and made a shiver race across her skin.

"I-I don't think I'm very good at this game, Lord St. Giles."

"Jack," he corrected. Although he was behind her, she could hear the smile in his voice as he added, "Shall we play something else, my dear?" as his hand squeezed her hip, which she felt all the way to her toes and which settled quite deeply in her womb.

Heavens, anything she would play with him would see her most decidedly ruined. "I-I don't…"

But his lips pressed against the side of her neck and Cassy couldn't finish her sentence or even think a coherent thought for that matter. His hands slid to her belly and urged her backwards until she was pressed against him. Heat pulsed through her and she couldn't help but rest her head against his chest.

He whispered against her neck, "You have captivated me since—"

Oscar barked out a warning.

"Cassy!" came Toby's voice in the corridor.

With a sigh, Lord St. Giles...er...Jack released his hold on Cassy, and he took a step away from her. "In here," he called to her brother.

Toby bounded inside the billiard room with Papa right on his heels. Her father frowned at her, and her brother gaped at the cue stick in Cassy's hand. "What are you doing with that?"

Good heavens! If Oscar hadn't barked when he had and Papa had found her and Jack just a moment ago, she'd have been done for. Cassy swallowed, hoping her voice would sound normal as she said, "Lord St. Giles offered to teach me how to play so I might beat Michael." Papa wouldn't like that, but it would be better than telling him that Jack had just been kissing her and holding her in his arms.

Toby cackled. "*I* can beat Michael."

"I'm certain there's something more appropriate you could be doing," Papa grumbled, his eyes darting from her to Lord St. Giles. "Certainly Mr. Hunt didn't summon *you* to Keyvnor."

Jack sighed very nonchalantly. "Offered to keep Lord Michael company."

Papa's brow lifted in disdain. "Then perhaps you should find *him* and refrain from teaching my daughter how to play billiards."

"Didn't mean to impose," Jack replied and he chanced a glance at Cassy.

Heavens, just a glance from him could make her warmer

than the hottest summer day. She could still feel the place on her neck where his lips had touched her, and Cassy wasn't certain if she'd ever feel anything so strongly for the rest of her life.

"Your mother is looking for you, Cassandra." That was hardly good news. Cassy couldn't remember the last time her mother was in a good humor.

"Is something wrong?" she managed to ask.

Papa heaved a sigh and flicked his gaze toward her poodle. "Seems Oscar broke a vase when he was running wild this morning. Your mother would like you to apologize to Lady Banfield."

Oh, no!

CHAPTER 7

"*I* just can't believe she wouldn't tell me," Michael complained for the umpteenth time.

But as the Beck brothers seemed to watch every move Lady Charlotte made, Jack had no trouble understanding why the girl had secretly made her way to the gypsy camp the day before. How unfortunate for the lady that Adam Vail had let that bit of information slip after his brother's funeral service.

"Perhaps she just wanted a bit of adventure," he said even though he knew it was pointless to say anything. Michael and Redgrave had been in a temper ever since they'd found out about their sister's excursion. "She never left Keyvnor land."

Michael blew out a breath as they entered the drawing room. "Those gypsies could have murdered her and hidden her body. And we'd have never known what happened to her."

That was the most ridiculous thing Jack had heard all day. He cast his friend an incredulous look. "You think Adam Vail is the sort to murder young ladies and hide their bodies?"

"Well...no, of course not," Michael grumbled. "But that's not the point. She didn't know Adam was there when she ran off to have her fortune told. She didn't even know Vail until yesterday. She just raced along headfirst without giving the situation proper thought or asking for permission."

And neither had Michael given proper thought to the fact that there was an audience in the drawing room when they'd entered. An audience of distant Banfield relations who were all staring at Michael and Jack with rapt attention.

Jack cleared his throat and nudged his friend in the side. Michael looked slightly purple and coughed into his hand, as though hoping the room at large would forget anything they might have overheard.

"Have you come to play whist?" One of Banfield's daughters asked. Lady Marjorie, Jack was fairly certain.

Possibly. Whist did seem like just the sort of entertainment Cassandra might attend. Lord Widcombe would probably deem this activity more appropriate than learning to play billiards. And as Jack had spent the rest of the day mesmerized by the memory of holding her in his arms, any activity that would allow him to spend time with her was an activity he deemed worth doing. "Is Lady Cassandra playing?" he asked, though he didn't see her in the drawing room.

Michael shot him a warning look, though Jack ignored his friend entirely.

Lady Marjorie frowned. "Um, I saw her earlier, but..."

Well, if Cassandra wasn't playing—

And then he heard the soft melodic sound of her voice behind him, just inside the threshold. He released a breath he hadn't realized he was holding. Jack turned on his heel to find Cassandra, her arm linked with her sister's. Her dark hair was knotted over one shoulder and the golden of her gown brought out the same color flecks in her eyes. She was stunning, still as breathtaking as the first moment he ever saw her. Should he live to be a hundred, Jack would never tire of gazing upon her beauty.

When Cassandra's eyes met his, a splash of pink stained her cheeks. Yes, she'd thought about him ever since their billiards lesson, he'd stake his life on it. Just like he'd thought about her. Jack let his gaze drink her in and was just about to reach his hand out to her when Lady Samantha tugged Cassandra toward the shy vicar's daughter Devon Lancaster had been half-chasing ever since they arrived.

"You have to play with me," Lady Samantha insisted. "Or someone else *will*."

That was mysterious. Cassandra glanced back at Jack, offering a silent apology with her smile, as she clearly couldn't abandon her sister.

"Well," Michael clapped a hand to Jack's back. "Guess that means you're stuck with me, old man."

"I might prefer the plague," Jack grumbled.

Michael laughed and gestured to a spot not too far away where Lancaster and Teddy Lockwood were already seated. At least at that table, he'd have a decent view of Cassandra.

～

Samantha seemed slightly annoyed with Cassy, not that Cassy could do anything about it. She had no mind for cards tonight and she'd have been hard pressed to concentrate on the game or anything else with Jack's eyes on her all evening. Each time she chanced a glance in his direction, he was watching her with that wicked smile of his that could melt her into a puddle on the floor.

"It would be nice if you might try focusing on the next hand," Samantha complained without heat.

Cassy straightened in her seat, prepared to do better. "We haven't lost all that much, Sam." Hardly anything at all really.

"What in the world?" came a familiar shrewish voice.

Samantha and Cassy winced in unison as their mother's shadow fell over the table.

"We're just playing, Mama," Cassy began.

"Playing for entertainment is one thing, but playing for money is gauche, Cassandra."

"We haven't lost all that much," Samantha echoed Cassy's earlier sentiment.

That, however, was the wrong thing to say as their mother's face turned an unattractive shade of red.

Mr. Lancaster appeared at their table in a flash. "Is everything all right?" he asked Miss Hawkins quietly.

"Of course not!" Mama snapped. "Miss Hawkins clearly doesn't understand that gently bred women do not gamble."

"You've lost money, then?" Mr. Lancaster frowned at Mama, and Cassy wished she could climb right under the table. It was gauche to gamble for money, but perfectly acceptable to embarrass one's children in front of everyone assembled. In front of Jack.

Mama's hands landed on her hips. "I would never consider wagering in cards. It's simply not done."

"How much did she lose?" Mr. Lancaster asked.

Miss Hawkins shrugged. "Her daughters, Lady Samantha and Lady Cassandra, played against Marjorie and me. We were only making small wagers."

Wonderful. Everyone would think Sam and Cassy were sore losers. If a hole would just open in the ground and swallow Cassy, she'd be forever grateful.

"Any wagers at all are inappropriate," Mama insisted. "And if you were from a decent family, you would know this."

Miss Hawkins pushed out of her seat, leaving her

winnings behind. "Marjorie, you can see to it that Lady Widcombe receives everything back." And then she made her exit with Mr. Lancaster quick on her heels.

Sam's face was flushed with color and Cassy was certain she looked the same. She couldn't even bear to glance in Jack's direction. But then he was there at the side of her table, standing right next to her mother.

"Lady Widcombe," he began. "You do look lovely this evening."

Mama blinked at him, then her brow scrunched up a bit. "Thank you, Lord St. Giles."

"Your nephew was just telling me that you play the harp."

Cassy glanced across the room at Michael who shrugged.

"It's been a while," Mama hedged.

Jack nodded. "I was afraid you'd say that. I noticed one in the music room a few days ago. My mother used to play and it made me wistful in my thoughts of her. I had hoped I might convince you to play a song or two."

"Oh." Mama's face brightened. "I didn't realize Her Grace played the harp."

"It's one of my fondest memories of her."

"Well, I suppose I could be convinced to play at least one song."

Jack beamed. "Only if you want to. I'd hate to impose."

"No, no," Mama insisted. "I would be honored."

And just that easily he'd managed to charm Mama and smooth her ruffled feathers. What accomplishments could Jack achieve if he set out to charm the world?

A small group departed for the music room and Jack offered Cassy his arm. She smiled up at him in amazement. "You are astonishing, Jack," she whispered as they trailed behind the others.

He winked at her. "Do go on, my dear. You can flatter me all night and I'll never stop you."

She couldn't help but laugh. "Did your mother really play the harp?"

A flash of sadness crossed his face. "She did," he said so softly that only she could hear him. "But I don't really remember her," he confided. "I wasn't even walking when she died. My sister Eleanor used to talk about her playing though. It's all just hearsay as I don't remember it myself."

How sad that he didn't remember his mother. As embarrassing as Mama was, Cassy couldn't imagine not having her around. "Someone else here must play as well. I heard one of the Hambly girls complaining about someone playing in the middle of the night."

"Not your mother?" Jack grinned.

"Mama would never do such—"

A coldness washed over Cassy as though frozen fingers had reached out and snatched her arm. She sucked in a breath and nearly froze in fear. Out of the corner of her eye, the man – the one in black who'd glared at her the day before – stood right beside her and then he faded away as though he'd never been there.

She let out a scream and hurled herself into Jack's arms.

CHAPTER 8

*W*hat the devil! Jack didn't even have time to mutter that phrase before Cassandra threw herself into his arms, shaking as though she'd been dipped into the frozen Irish Sea.

Everyone in their small party came to a stop. And Jack couldn't really blame them. She had let out an ear-piercing scream. But he held her close and whispered, "I'm here, Cassandra. It's all right. I'm here."

"What in the world?" Lady Widcombe demanded, making her way through the crowd to yank her daughter out of Jack's arms. He felt the loss instantly.

Cassandra was still shaking and Jack would have done anything to hold her once more and try to soothe whatever was wrong.

"Th-th-the man in black," she stuttered. "H-h-he grabbed me, a-a-and then he vanished and—"

Lady Widcombe released a world-weary sigh. "Not again, Cassandra," she hissed. "You are making a scene."

"I'll take her back to her chambers," Lady Samantha offered.

But the panicked expression in Cassandra's eyes tore at Jack's heart. There was nothing he could do. He couldn't offer to escort Cassandra to her chambers, he couldn't suggest she not retire when she was clearly upset, he couldn't do anything except stand there with the rest of the audience assembled around them.

"I saw him!" Cassandra insisted. "H-he touched my arm."

Her sister took her hand and began to lead her in the opposite direction.

"He did! He touched me!"

Jack watched the Priske sisters disappear around the corner and a pall fell over the assembled group. Cassandra almost sounded mad. Not almost mad. If he wasn't half-way in love with her, she'd sound quite mad. But...Well, he *was* half-way in love with her. He had been for some time. And he wasn't sure if he'd ever felt as helpless as he did in that moment. No amount of luck or charisma could change what had just happened in the corridor. And no amount of fortune or charm could help Cassandra. There was absolutely nothing he could do. Damn it all.

"Do you think *she* was the one screaming in the middle of the night?" Hal Mort, Viscount Blackwater, asked; and Jack was quite tempted to smash his fist in the fellow's face, even if he was an old friend.

"I'm terribly sorry about that," Lady Widcombe apologized, her round face flushed and her voice trembling slightly.

"With all the stories surrounding Keyvnor, anyone might be shaken to be here," Teddy Lockwood offered.

"Indeed," Jack agreed, grateful to Lockwood for giving Cassandra an excuse. It might not be the best excuse, but it would do. "Been on edge a bit myself," he lied. Then he flashed a weary smile toward Lady Widcombe. "Might I impose upon you to pay the harp another time, my lady? I think I may retire early this evening."

"Yes, yes, of course, Lord St. Giles. I am terribly sorry if Cassandra has upset you."

He was more worried than upset, but accepted the lady's words versus discussing the semantics of the situation. "I do appreciate it."

Without a glance back over his shoulder, Jack started for the other end of the castle, hoping he could catch up to Cassandra and her sister. Honestly, shouldn't her mother be more concerned than she was? He didn't remember his own mother, but his oldest sister Helen had been the doting sort. If any of their sisters had behaved the way Cassandra had just now, Helen would have taken on the motherly role and seen to their sister's wellbeing no matter what else was happening. While it was nice Lady Samantha was seeing to Cassandra, the ladies did have a mother who was alive and well, and...Well, Lady Widcombe should seem more concerned than she was.

If—

"Jack!" came a familiar voice behind him, and Jack glanced back over his shoulder to find Lockwood and Blackwater following in his wake.

"Not the best time at the moment."

Lockwood sighed. "Yes, I have a good idea where you're headed, but perhaps you shouldn't chase after the girl right now."

He wasn't chasing after Cassandra...Well, technically, he *was* chasing after her to make sure she was all right. But he wasn't chasing her skirts at the moment. "You both can keep your own council on the matter."

Blackwater looked slightly uncomfortable. "Madness *does* run in the family, Jack—"

Lockwood balled his hand into a fist and glared at the

viscount. "That's nothing but a ridiculous tale. The madness isn't hereditary. Lady Claire is quite sane."

"We both know it is," Blackwater countered. "Both her mother *and* her aunt suffered from it. Who's to say Lady Cassandra..."

Who was to say Cassandra wasn't just as mad as the ladies in Claire Deering's family? Jack heaved an irritated sigh.

And Lockwood looked quite murderous all of a sudden. "Now see here," he began.

"Lady Cassandra is related to the late-earl, not his wife." Jack cut him off, not having the patience or inclination to engage in this conversation. "There's no madness in *her* family." Though her mother might be mad with the total lack of concern she'd shown for her daughter. Jack opted, however, not to say as much to his friends.

"Just want you to be careful," Blackwater added.

"I appreciate your concern." But he really needed to catch Cassandra and her sister before all trace of them was gone. He turned his back on his friends and started down the corridor where the Priske sisters had departed.

He rounded the corner and...There was no sign of either lady. Damn Lockwood and Blackwater straight to the devil. They'd delayed him just long enough for him to loose the girls. And then he heard a dog bark.

Oscar! Perfect!

Jack hurried toward the sound, certain the poodle would be following after Cassandra and her sister, but the dog was sitting in the corridor barking at the wall. Hardly helpful.

"Oscar," Jack called. "Where's your lady?"

The poodle stood up and wagged his tail.

"Where's Cassandra?" Jack tried again. "Find Cassandra."

But the little dog raced toward Jack and sat at his feet, looking up at him as though hoping for a treat.

Damn it all, Jack would need to travel the corridors of

Keyvnor with dog treats in his pockets from here on out. He gestured down the corridor. "Go find Cassandra."

Oscar barked, but made no effort to move.

"If I get you a treat from the kitchens, will you take me to your lady's chambers?" he asked and then shook his head for sounding like a fool. Somehow, Jack had been reduced to asking a dog for help and having to bribe the little thing with treats.

~

*C*assy wasn't mad. She wasn't. That man all in black *had* touched her and then he *had* disappeared! She hadn't imagined it, had she? Not like she had imagined Grandpapa, right? No, of course not. She shook her head at the idea. That man...er...ghost or whatever or whoever he was had touched her! She'd felt his frosty touch on her arm. She'd never forget that feeling as long as she lived.

Shivering slightly at the memory, she pulled her wrapper tighter around her. So, she wasn't mad, but it was more than maddening that no one believed her. For heaven's sake, why would she make up a story like that?

The candle against the far wall flickered and Cassy padded across the rug to use the flame to light another candle. After all, she couldn't have too much light. Not tonight, perhaps not ever. If she had a thousand candles at her disposal, she was quite certain she'd light every single one of them to—

A familiar scratching sound came from the door, not a servant trying to get her attention. No, that insistent scratch could only come from Oscar. Thank heavens! She did not relish being in her chambers alone now that her sister was gone. Sam had been kind to sit with her a while and make sure Cassy's heart had returned to a more sedate pace, but she wouldn't truly be herself until she left the walls of Keyvnor behind her for good.

But even if no one else believed her about the man in black or any of the other strangeness at Keyvnor, Oscar believed her. He'd sensed the same things she had. At least she thought he did.

Cassy crossed the room to open the door for her poodle, but...

Jack stood in the corridor alongside her dog. Oscar raced inside her chambers and promptly hopped up onto her bed, at least she assumed he did from the sound of the bed springs squeaking behind her; but Cassy didn't dare pull her gaze away from Jack. Was he really there?

"What are you doing here?" She had, after all, been quite certain he'd wash his hands completely of her after this evening's incident. He had made it very clear that he didn't believe in such things as ghosts or spirits. And one of those things he didn't believe in had reached out and grabbed Cassy's arm.

"I needed to make sure you're all right."

A shiver raced across her spine at the memory of the man in black's cold fingers. "I won't be all right until I leave here."

Jack frowned slightly. "May I come in?"

To her chambers? Cassy's mouth fell open. She was already in her nightrail and wrapper. Was he trying to ruin her? "I don't think—"

"I don't think we should have a conversation like this." He gestured to her in her chambers and him in the corridor. "Someone could come upon us, and that wouldn't look proper at all."

Not that having him in her chambers was proper either. In fact it was far from it, but...Well, no one would know if he was inside, right? Not if they didn't see him enter or leave. "No one saw you, did they?"

"I do hope not." He flashed her that charming smile that could melt her insides. "I looked like quite the fool begging Oscar to lead me to you. We had to make a stop at the kitchens. He's not a fan of mutton. Did you know?"

How was it possible he managed to make her laugh, even now when she felt so alone and terrified? "You've spoiled him with pheasant." Cassy said as she opened her door wide enough for the baron to enter her borrowed set of rooms.

Just as soon as he closed the door behind him, Jack pulled her into his embrace. Cassy breathed in the scent of his shaving lotion and welcomed the heat of him against her skin. Heavens! Was there anywhere in the world that felt safer than being in his arms?

"Tell me what happened," he finally said.

But she didn't want to talk about the man in black and she didn't want to think about him either. "You won't believe me."

"Cassandra," he urged and tipped her chin up so she had to meet his silvery eyes.

And looking so deeply into his depths did make her knees weak. How long would that last? Would he run as far away from her as he could once she told him everything she saw? "You were right there, Jack. Everyone was right there, but..." She winced, hating the memory of everyone staring at her as though she was a Bedlamite. And she didn't want to see that look in his eyes so she focused on his lips instead.

"But?" he echoed.

"You were right there, but you didn't see him. No one else saw him. But he *was* there. The same man from the window. The one who glared at me as we arrived. He was right there and he touched my arm."

Jack frowned, clearly not believing her. She hadn't thought that he would, though she had foolishly hoped that he might. But that frown said otherwise.

Cassy pushed out of his arms and the chill of her chambers swirled back around her. "I don't expect you to believe me."

"I *was* there," he said slowly. "But I didn't see any man, ghostly or otherwise, touch you. It could have been a draft or—"

"It wasn't a draft!" she insisted. "I saw him. I saw him with my two eyes and he grabbed me." Cassy turned back toward her bed and sat on the edge. "I can still feel an iciness where his fingers curled around my arm. I'll never forget how that felt."

Oscar plodded across the counterpane and dropped down beside her. What a true friend her poodle was. Loyal to a fault, even if she was bound for Bedlam.

Jack heaved a sigh and crossed the room. He sat on the edge of her bed next to Oscar and looked at her with such concern it almost broke her heart.

"I know you think I'm mad."

He reached his hand out and captured hers. "On the contrary, I've always thought you were the most levelheaded girl."

"Until now."

His silvery eyes held her gaze and warmth settled very closely to her heart. "If you say you saw something, then you saw something."

As though a weight she didn't know she was carrying was lifted off her shoulders by those words, Cassy couldn't help but throw her arms around Jack's neck. Oscar grumbled as he moved out of the way, but she paid her pet very little attention. How could she think about anything other than the fact that Jack Hazelwood believed her?

The heat of his hands nearly seared her though her nightrail and wrap as he held her close against the stone wall of his chest. Heavens! He really shouldn't be there. If anyone ever saw them like this…

"Jack," she whispered. "You should leave before someone discovers you're here."

He pulled back slightly from her. "Do you want me to leave?"

She never wanted him to leave. She felt safe when she was with him, but he couldn't stay in her chambers with her. "If my father knew you were in here…"

"That's not what I asked." His eyes bore into hers once more. "Do *you* want me to leave, Cassandra?"

Her cheeks stung with heat. "What I want is inconsequential."

"Not to me."

Cassy dropped her gaze and stared at his cravat. "I feel safe with you. Of course, I wish you could stay. But that would—"

"I'll leave in the morning before your maid comes for you. No one will know I was here."

"You're mad," she breathed out, meeting his eyes once more.

That devilish smile teased at the corners of Jack's lips. "We might both be. But I'm not leaving you."

CHAPTER 9

Of all the times Jack had envisioned having Cassandra Priske in bed beside him, he'd never once thought he'd be fully dressed. Well, he was *almost* fully dressed. He was missing his cravat, jacket and waistcoat, but other than that, he was quite properly attired. If one could be quite properly attired and in bed with an innocent girl. And though on any other given night, he'd be rather focused on seduction, tonight he just wanted to hold her against him and soothe away all her fears. Besides, seduction would come soon enough, right after he married her. And he had no doubt that he was going to marry her.

Of course, marriage had not been his intent when he'd followed Michael to Keyvnor and then goaded Lockwood, Blackwater and Lancaster into joining them in Cornwall. Or perhaps it was. He'd chased Cassandra Priske for so long, and he supposed he never really thought about what would happen when he caught her. Perhaps he'd known all along that she'd be his baroness, someday his duchess. He may have known that very first time he'd seen her, heard her defend a girl more unfortunate than herself with such compassion, he'd felt it in his soul.

The fact that he could have such thoughts on marriage now and not be terrified in the least seemed to be proof enough that his mind had caught up with what his heart had known all along. He didn't just want Cassandra in his arms or in his bed, he wanted her there always and in every other part of his life.

From her side of the bed, Cassandra glanced back over her shoulder at him. "Do you have enough room?"

He might, if Oscar wasn't pressed against his legs. He slid her poodle to the other side of the bed with his foot. "Come let me hold you."

Even in the fading candlelight, the blush on her cheeks caught his notice. Would she always blush like that? Even when she wasn't so innocent? Even after a dozen years with him? After they had a brood of their own? He rather hoped she would. It was endearing, enchanting and called to him like nothing ever had.

Cassandra snuggled against him and Jack buried his face in her dark locks that he'd wanted to touch for so long. He breathed in the soft lilac scent of her and couldn't help but sigh.

"Jack," she whispered, and his cock twitched in reaction.

"Mmm," he breathed against her.

"Tell me something."

"Something?"

She shrugged in his arms. "Anything. Something that will take my mind off Keyvnor and swarthy looking ghosts."

Oh, he could take her mind off Keyvnor and he'd enjoy every second of doing so. But he truly hadn't come to her chambers to seduce her, and the last thing he wanted to do was take advantage of her now that he was there.

"Tell me something about you. Something I don't know."

He smiled even though she couldn't see him. "Well, I am *the* most dashing man in all of England."

"And so very modest," she said, and he could hear the smile in her voice. "But I said tell me something I don't know."

Jack supposed it was good she agreed that he was dashing, but instead of reveling in that fact, he decided he could start with the basics to keep her mind off everything else. "I've three older sisters, all of whom I love dearly; but I'm closest to Marianne."

"Marianne?" she echoed.

"The youngest of the three." And the most delicate of them all. "You'd like her, I think." Or at the very least she wouldn't shun his sister. That he was certain of. He still remembered how ardently she'd defended that unfortunate Miss Keeting, and knew, without a doubt, that she would accept Marianne without question.

"What's she like?" Cassandra asked softly.

"She's the gentlest of souls. Kindhearted. Afraid of her own shadow most of the time."

"I'm *not* afraid of my own shadow," Cassandra grumbled.

Jack couldn't help but laugh as he squeezed her tighter. "No, no, no. I wasn't talking about ghosts, my dear. I didn't mean you at all. Marianne is...Well, our father can be less than warm on a good day, and he's been particularly harsh with her over the years. I believe he's made her more nervous and skittish than she would have been otherwise."

If it hadn't been for Father's unkind comments, always barked and with an audience present, Jack was certain Marianne would have grown out of her stuttering. In fact, she was better when Father wasn't around, constantly passing judgment on her, constantly reminding her that she did not measure up to his ducal standards.

Cassandra shifted in his arms and looked up at him. "She's afraid of him?"

"Everyone is a little afraid of him, but he has a tendency to prey on the weak, and in our family, that was always Marianne." Jack sighed, not really having divulged this sort of thing to anyone before. His sisters knew the fact as well as he did, so there was no reason to discuss it with them. He'd never thought to mention his father to any of his friends. Everyone, he was certain, had their own familial crosses to bear. "And he handpicked a husband for her who would continue his tyranny. It's by God's grace the man is gone and Marianne is free. Mostly."

"Mostly?" she asked, her brow scrunched with worry.

"Father does still interfere in her life, in her son's life from time to time. But I do what I can to keep him at bay." Jack shrugged slightly. "He's not as young as he used to be. And his annoyance with me takes most of his energy these days."

She seemed to bite back a smile at that, and Jack wondered which tale of his exploits she must be thinking of. Probably better not to know.

Then she sobered a bit. "You've mentioned your father in passing before," she began. "Is he truly so awful?"

His Grace was heartless and cruel on any given day. He reveled in tormenting each of his children, which was why Jack was quite happy to wear his rakish reputation for all to see as it annoyed the old man to no end. There was something quite satisfying in seeing the veins in his father's neck pulse with frustration as he berated Jack. "The happiest day of my life was the day I was sent off to Eton," he confided. It was such a relief to be out from under his father's roof and with other boys his age. It was the first time in Jack's life he'd felt as though he could take a breath of air, as though he'd gone through the first twelve years of his life without truly breathing at all. "Sadly, there was no escape for my sisters until they each married. Helen and June are both happily settled, and now that Fitzhugh is gone, Marianne is happier than she was. When my father is finally gone, I'll make certain she's as happy as she can be."

Cassandra smiled softly up at him. "You care about her very much."

"I love her. I want her have all the happiness she deserves."

"You know, I do believe there's much more to you than I originally thought, Jack Hazelwood."

He winked at her. "Well, I'm still a dangerous rake, Cassandra Priske, don't forget that."

"That would be impossible to forget." She giggled and the sound of her laugh swirled around his heart. "And you should call me Cassy. My friends all call me that."

"Am I your friend?" he asked.

She laughed again. "You *are* in my bed. I'm not sure how much closer of friends we could be."

Jack pressed his lips to hers, desire and need coursing through his veins. She was pressed against the length of him, her breasts against his chest, her belly against his straining cock, her legs entwined with his. It would be so incredibly simple to have her now, but not like this. She deserved better than this. She deserved everything he could give her and more.

He lifted his head and her hazel eyes twinkled even in the fading candlelight, so full of trust and wonder. God in heaven, he did love her, there was no question about that.

"I don't want to be your friend," he said, his voice coming out as a growl to his own ears. "I want so much more than that, Cassy. But not tonight, not here in this place. When I do make love to you, I want everything to be perfect, and I don't intend on ever letting you leave."

She sighed and snuggled closer to him, resting her hand above his heart. He might have meant to take her mind off the events at Keyvnor, but she had distracted him just as easily.

～

*J*ack Hazelwood's kiss was nothing short of magical. Cassy had never felt so wanted, so adored, so cared for in all her life. She nestled next to him and breathed in the scent of his sandalwood lotion and sighed against his neck.

When I do make love to you, I want everything to be perfect, and I don't intend on ever letting you leave.

Those words echoed over and over in her mind as Jack held her close, his touch warming every inch of her and making her core pulse with an urgency she didn't truly understand. She'd asked him to distract her, and she wasn't certain she'd ever be able to think about anything else for the rest of her life.

When I do make love to you, I want everything to be perfect, and I don't intend on ever letting you leave.

If his kiss was magical, what more was he promising her? And were his words a proposal of sorts? Jack didn't seem like the marrying sort, not by any stretch of the imagination. But what else could he have meant?

When I do make love to you, I want everything to be perfect, and I don't...

Cassy woke with a start and sat up with a jolt. A coldness swept over her and even in the darkness, she could see her breath as she breathed out.

"Cassy?" Jack said from the bed beside her. "Are you all right?"

Was she? Cassy glanced around her chambers. She didn't

see anything ghostly, but the coldness seemed to seep straight into her bones. "Aren't you freezing?" she whispered.

"Lay back down," he said tiredly. "I'll keep you warm."

She snuggled down beneath the counterpane and Jack held her close once more, sending a comfortable warmth back over her skin. "I can't wait to leave this place," she muttered.

Jack's lips grazed the side of her neck, heating her more than his hold had done. "Don't be in such a hurry to leave me, love."

CHAPTER 10

True to his word, Jack slid from Cassy's chambers as the first bit of color stained the horizon. It was a monumental feat leaving the comfort of her warm bed, of her lithe form pressed so perfectly against his, to head out into the chilly corridors of Castle Keyvnor.

At least he'd left her sleeping peacefully. He smiled as he thought about her wrapped up in her counterpane as he'd left and was glad he'd been able to bring her a little solace through the night.

Jack rounded a corner and nearly ran right into Redgrave of all the damned people at Keyvnor. "Beg your pardon," he said and tried to step around Cassy's overprotective cousin.

"You're up early." Redgrave narrowed his eyes on Jack.

"Yes, well, no need to keep Town hours when one isn't in Town." Jack moved again to pass the viscount, who stepped into his path once more.

"Isn't that the same jacket and waistcoat you wore yesterday?"

Damn the man straight to hell. Jack forced a grin to his face as he replied wryly, "I had no idea you kept such a keen eye focused on *my* fashion, Redgrave. I'm sure my tailor would be honored. Shall I send you his direction?"

"Where've you been?" the humorless viscount returned.

Jack heaved a sigh. "Long night, couldn't sleep and ended up walking the castle."

"Alone?"

The obnoxious prig.

Jack shrugged. "To hear Michael tell it, no one is ever truly alone at Keyvnor."

The man heaved an irritated sigh. How unpleasant it must be to be so serious all the time. If he'd just get his knob polished more often, he'd probably be a much more likable fellow. Probably.

"Now see, here, St. Giles," Redgrave finally began, "I don't care one whit that the female half of the species seems to find you charming for some reason. But do keep your distance from my sister and my cousins."

"You've already said as much." Jack breathed out a sigh of his own. "I'm sure there's some other fellow wandering about that you could be threatening in my stead. Perhaps one who hasn't already heard your dire warnings." He then pushed the viscount aside. "Do excuse me."

Time to change clothes before anyone else spotted him in yesterday's jacket and waistcoat.

~

*H*eavens! It was freezing. Cassy snuggled deeper under her covers, missing the comfort of Jack's warmth. She had no idea how long he'd been gone, just that he wasn't there any longer and the heat he'd brought with him last night had long since vanished. She sighed at the memory of being held against him, the strength of his chest at her back and safety of his arms wrapped around her. He was, in a word, perfect.

"Absolutely perfect," she whispered to the empty room. "Don't you think so, Oscar?"

But there was no little black bundle of fluff at the foot of the bed like there usually was. Cassy frowned as she stretched her arms over her head to wake up.

"Oscar?" she said again.

But there was no barking, no whining, no thump of an overzealous tail. Usually her little poodle woke her quite early so he could be let outside, but...Well, where in the world *was* Oscar? He should have had her up hours ago.

Cassy pushed up on her elbows and scanned her borrowed chambers. "Oscar!"

Where could he be? He'd been with Jack and her last night. She knew that for a fact, but...*Jack!* He must have taken Oscar with him when he left so she could sleep. The wonderful man.

A smile spread across her face as she collapsed back against her pillows. Yes, perfect. Jack was most definitely perfect.

After a moment, she pushed the counterpane from her and scrambled out of bed and over to the bell pull in the corner of her chambers. Time to bathe and dress and hurry down to the breakfast room in hopes of finding Jack and Oscar.

Although after a quick glance out the window while she waited for Betsy to attend her, Cassy noticed the sun was quite high in the sky. She'd already slept through breakfast, most definitely.

~

*A*s Devon Lancaster finished his brandy and departed the billiards room for parts unknown, Jack decided quite fervently that his friend had lost his mind. After all, the man was in desperate need of an heiress bride, and while there were several ladies in residence at Keyvnor who would do nicely, Lancaster had spent nearly every waking moment this last week mooning over a penniless vicar's daughter instead. It was almost as though he *wanted* to live in a poor house.

How fortunate Jack was that marrying for money was not something he'd ever had to contemplate for himself. With as tightfisted as his father was, the coffers of the Margate dukedom would be near to overflowing by the time he did finally inherit the title.

Jack lined up a shot, even though he was now quite alone in the room, and struck the ball with his stick. The ball bounced off the far cushion and rolled back toward him rather nicely.

There was no harm in practicing for a bit, especially as Lancaster, Lockwood and Blackwater were otherwise engaged, and he had no idea where Michael had hidden himself. He'd seen his friend at breakfast, but sometime that afternoon the man had disappeared. So what else was Jack to do but line up his shots and perfect his game while he waited for Cassy to come down for the day? Honestly, it was later than he'd expected, but as she'd tossed and turned most of the night, he did hope she was resting peacefully.

He lined up the white ball again.

"Have you seen Oscar?" Toby Priske asked from the threshold just as Jack struck the cue ball, which promptly jumped the cushion, thudded onto the rug and rolled toward the little boy.

"Oscar?" Jack straightened and placed his stick on the billiard table.

"Cassy's dog," the boy replied as he snatched the cue ball up in his hand. "Can't seem to find the little beast anywhere."

He was probably knocking over more vases somewhere in Keyvnor that Cassy would have to apologize for later. "Sorry. Haven't seen him. How long has he been—"

And then Cassy appeared in the doorway beside her brother, like a vision come to life. Sleeping beauty finally awakes. "Jack," she breathed out. Her golden gown with a nicely scooped bodice made the flecks in her hazel eyes shine ever so brightly. On his life, Jack had never seen a prettier girl, and she was just as beautiful inside as she was out.

"You can't find Oscar?" he asked, unable to pull his gaze from her.

"I was hoping—" she glanced down at her little brother as though wishing he wasn't there "—you might have seen him this *morning.*"

That morning when he left her bedchamber? Had her poodle been missing all that time? Jack tried to remember seeing the little ball of fluff, but nothing popped to mind. "I don't recall seeing him," he said slowly. Though he probably wouldn't have noticed Oscar one way or the other as his mind had been firmly focused on the girl whose bed he'd just slipped from. "I did bump into Redgrave this morning. Perhaps he spotted him."

She winced. "Anthony saw you?"

Not coming out of her room, but Jack couldn't say those exact words , not with her little brother present. "We chatted while I was walking the castle." Hopefully that was enough to put her worry at rest.

She smiled slightly. "Well, I would ask him, but I haven't seen any of my cousins today."

Neither had Jack, not since breakfast. "I'm happy to help

you look for the little fellow. Perhaps a bit of pheasant might do the trick."

"Thank you," she said softly.

"Where have you looked?" Jack asked as he started for the threshold and offered Cassy his arm.

"I've gone through all the public rooms," she replied. "There's no sign of him."

Jack gestured to Toby. "You take the bedchambers. He might have gotten trapped if a maid shut him in someone's chamber by accident."

"You want me to go into people's bedchambers?" The boy gaped at him.

"It would be much more scandalous if either your sister or I did so."

Toby blew out a breath. "Mother will be furious if I get caught."

"Then try not to get caught," Cassy said. "You're clever enough at home. What if poor Oscar is trapped in someone's chambers?"

CHAPTER 11

"Oscar!" Cassy stepped from the castle into the gardens with Jack at her side. She shivered slightly at the ominous clouds that always seemed to hover over this corner of Cornwall.

"Here, Oscar!" Jack called, refocusing Cassy on the matter at hand. "I have that pheasant you love."

Cassy's stomach knotted into a ball. What in the world could have happened to her poodle? "Did you remember seeing him at all this morning?" Cassy asked as she led Jack toward the hedge maze. Oscar could have gotten lost in the maze and not been able to find his way out. He was probably terrified if that's where he was.

"I didn't notice him, Cassy," Jack said quietly. "I was preoccupied with not waking you and making an escape before anyone discovered me."

Well, she supposed that made sense, though it was hardly the news she'd hoped for. "He always wakes me first thing to go outside. I thought you must have taken him out for me."

"Sorry, love." He squeezed her fingers and warmth shot through her. "But he's here somewhere. We'll find him."

"You'll remember the way out, won't you?" she asked as they took their first turn around a hedge. She'd never been the most directionally adept. Perhaps she and Oscar had that in common.

"Today I'll remember," he promised.

That made her stop in her tracks and she looked up at him. "Today?"

He winked at her and that familiar warmth within her spread even further. "We might *want* to get lost in here tomorrow. And then, I daresay, I shan't be able to recall the way out."

She couldn't help it. She laughed. Even with Oscar gone and her nerves on edge. He had the ability to lighten her heart, the charming scoundrel. "I'm certain I must always be on my toes with you, Jack."

"I'd much rather have you in my arms."

And she'd much rather be there instead of searching for her lost dog. "Will you stay with me again tonight?" she asked and was certain her cheeks must be red as an apple. Heavens! What had gotten into her? How forward had she become?

"There's nowhere else I'd rather be." He drew her to a stop and pulled her into his arms. "Did you know you've captivated me since the first moment I saw you?"

She remembered the intensity in his gaze when they'd first met. She'd never felt anything like it before in her life. "The Weatherings' ball," she whispered.

His grey eyes twinkled just a bit. "Since the first time I *saw* you, love, not the first time I met you."

He'd seen her before that night? She'd had no idea. Had she seen him before, she was certain she'd have remembered.

"Vauxhall gardens," he answered her unasked question. "You were strolling down the south walk with your cousin and—" he shrugged "—some willowy blonde, if my memory serves me—"

Vauxhall? She hadn't attended anything at the gardens during the last season, but the previous season before she and Charlotte had been guests of Lady Lydia Allwood and her family on one occasion.

"—Though honestly, I only vividly remember you from that night. The single most beautiful girl I've ever seen."

Cassy's breath caught in her throat. "I barely remember that evening."

"I'll never forget it," he replied. "Neither Ashbrooke nor Blackwater knew who you were, which made it quite impossible to get an introduction. And then another girl walked past, going the other direction. A red birthmark covered half of her face."

"Miss Keeting," Cassy replied. She did remember the scene. The poor girl was so terribly shy and self-conscious, and Lydia had been quite vicious that evening. How embarrassing that Jack had witnessed that particular exchange.

Jack nodded. "The blonde you were with asked how the girl had the nerve to show her face in public."

She'd actually said that Miss Keeting should hide her face to keep from scaring the small children walking the pleasure gardens. Cassy winced at the memory. "Lydia can be cruel." Which was the main reason she hadn't socialized with the lady in well over a year.

"But not you," he said softly. "You defended the girl quite determinedly. She couldn't have found a better champion than you that evening."

"Miss Keeting's shy, but a very sweet girl."

"And so are you." His silvery gaze bore into hers. "Beautiful inside and out. I've been captivated by you since that evening. Took me until the next season to discover your name. If I'd known you were Michael's cousin, I'd have found you much quicker."

Had he really been searching for her since that night at Vauxhall? Cassy swallowed nervously.

"Then, of course, you hid from me and—"

"I didn't hide," she protested.

Jack grinned as he tucked a strand of her hair behind her ear. "What would you call it?"

They both knew she'd hidden from him, there was no point in pressing the lie. "You terrified me."

His brow furrowed. "*I* terrified you?"

"No one ever looked at me the way you did." Cassy's gaze dropped to his cravat. "And you *do* have a certain reputation. I was terrified of what I might be led to do if I spent any time in your company."

He leaned forward and brushed his lips across her brow. "On my life, I've only ever had honorable intentions where you're concerned."

Before Cassy could reply to that, she heard a rustling in the hedge up ahead. Oscar! It must be! "Did you hear that?" she asked, stepping out of Jack's embrace.

"Did I hear what?"

The hedge rustled again. It had to be her poodle.

"Oscar!" she called darting around the hedge and then around the next one and then... blocking her path was the awful, swarthy looking man in black. His glare sent a shiver racing down her spine and a chill straight to her bones.

Cassy screamed, turned on her heel, and ran back toward where she'd left Jack, but he wasn't there. At least, she thought she'd run back to where she'd left him. "Jack!"

A chilly darkness hovered over her. The swarthy man in black reached down toward her, and Cassy screamed one more time as she fell to her knees and covered her head with both arms.

◦

*G*ood God! Where the devil was she? Cassy had been there one moment and gone the next. By the time she bolted away and Jack chased after her, she'd disappeared, somewhere in the maze. Who would've thought so slight a girl could move so quickly in a dress?

"Jack!" she screamed from somewhere in the hedges. She couldn't be too far away. But how to find her?

"Cassy!" he called back and hurried toward the sound of her voice, which lead to a dead end. Damn the bloody maze.

She was whimpering, somewhere close by. Jack spun on his heel and rushed back the way he'd come and chose a different path. Her whimpering became louder. He rounded the next hedge and there she was, cowering in a ball in a corner of the maze, shivering.

Good God!

"Cassy!" Jack raced to her. "Sweetheart," he said more softly when she hadn't lifted her head to see him. Still she didn't seem to hear him, so he sank to his haunches and lifted his hand out to touch her arm.

The moment his skin touched hers, she yelped and shrunk against the hedge.

What the devil?

"Cassy," he tried again, more urgently. "Love, what's wrong?"

Finally, she lifted her head up and her eyes looked wild. "Get away from me."

Jack pulled his hand back from her, even though he wanted to wrap his arms around her and comfort whatever was wrong. "Cassy, what is it, love?"

"Make him stay away from me, Jack," she sobbed.

Jack glanced over his shoulder but there was no one there. "Sweetheart, it's just us." Wasn't it?

But Cassy shook her head stubbornly. "He's here. He was *just* here, Jack."

He? Who? "Oscar?" he asked, feeling like a dolt and beyond helpless.

And then she cried even harder. "Oscar! *He's* done something to Oscar, Jack. I know it."

"Who?" he asked, reaching his hand out to her one more time.

"The m-man in bl-black," she managed between sobs.

The *ghost* she was convinced had grabbed her last night? A sickening feeling washed over Jack.

Madness does run in the family. Blackwater's warning from the night before echoed in his ears. Jack shook the thought from his mind. Cassy wasn't a blood relation to Lady Claire Deering's family. Even so...

He'd known Lady Claire nearly all of his life. The lady was frightened to death that madness would take her someday like it had her mother and aunt. And yet he'd never thought her mad, not even one day of their acquaintance. But Cassy...he couldn't make himself finish that thought. She couldn't be mad. There had to be some other explanation...

An explanation that involved glaring ghosts that only *she* could see? No one with a rational mind could accept such a thing. It wasn't even in the realm of possibilities. Jack's sickening feeling worsened.

"Come on, sweetheart," he said gently. "Let's get you back inside the castle."

"He's done something to Oscar. W-we have to find Oscar."

Jack nodded in agreement. "Aye, I'll find him. But let's get you out of here for now, shall we?" And then he scooped her up in his arms and pushed back to his feet before she could object.

She rested her head against his shoulder as he navigated

the maze. Her lilac scent drifted up to him and it nearly broke his heart. He'd chased after her, lusted after her, fallen completely in love with her. He'd been convinced she was *the* lady he was going to live the rest of his life with. But had he been so in love with her that he'd been blind to the deficiencies of her sanity? He'd seen the way Claire's father, the Marquess of Brauning, had suffered through his wife's madness. That wasn't a life he wanted for himself.

Jack's heart twisted in his chest as he navigated the maze and stepped back into the south gardens. Once in the clearing, he spotted Lord Widcombe near the castle's south entrance. When the earl's gaze locked with Jack's, a hardened expression settled on his face.

"What *are* you doing with my daughter?" the man bellowed, stomping in Jack and Cassy's direction.

"She got lost in the maze," Jack tried to explain. "She's frightened, and—"

"Perhaps I haven't been direct enough, St. Giles." Lord Widcombe snatched Cassy from Jack's arms and he felt the loss instantly. "I do not want a man of your character associating with my daughter."

"P-papa," Cassy began in between sobs. "There's a ghost and—"

The earl's face looked hard as stone. "Not one more word out of you."

And then Widcombe turned on his heel and started back inside the castle, leaving Jack to stare after the pair, wondering if he'd just been saved from a life with Cassy or condemned to a life without her.

No matter how much he wished Cassy was with him and that she was as sane as Jack had always thought her to be, he *had* promised to find Oscar. And searching for her dog would be a most needed distraction.

CHAPTER 12

*C*assy couldn't help but sob into her pillow. She was shaken right to her core. She could still feel the cool darkness that had swept over her in the maze. It was as though the man in black still clung to her skin and she couldn't shake the feeling of him surrounding her.

"I have never been more embarrassed by anyone in my life than I have *you* over the last two days," Mama shrieked. "I have had quite enough of this ghost nonsense, Cassandra. Quite enough."

So had Cassy. She was more than ready to leave Castle Keyvnor and its ghosts, especially the ominous man in black, far behind her. Of course, she couldn't stop sobbing long enough to even defend herself, not that it would matter. Mama would hear nothing of it anyway.

"Nonsense, indeed," Papa agreed with an irritable growl to his voice. "And so is this flirtation you've been engaging in with Lord St. Giles. Do you want to be ruined, Cassandra?"

Jack wasn't trying to ruin her. Her father would never convince her of that. He was the only one who believed her.

Well, Jack and Oscar. Where *was* Oscar? What had that awful man in black done with her poodle? Another sob escaped her.

"Don't be hasty, Peter," Mama said quickly. "He's *Margate*'s son."

Papa blew out a frustrated breath. "He's a degenerate."

"Who will be a *duke* someday," Mama continued. "Cassy's been fortunate he's looked past her ridiculous outbursts the last few days. She could do worse, especially if anyone outside these walls should ever find out about her behavior since we've been here."

Papa snorted. "You didn't see the look of relief he sported when I took Cassandra from him. He thinks she's mad. I could see it in his eyes."

That wasn't true, was it? Cassy sucked in a sob. It couldn't be true. Her parents might think she was mad, but not Jack. "H-he believes me, Papa." He'd said as much, after all.

The dismissive expression on her father's face chilled Cassy to her bones. "Did he tell you that in exchange for taking certain liberties, Cassandra?"

What? That couldn't be true. Could it? What if it was? She knew Jack hadn't believed in ghosts when he arrived at Keyvnor. But last night...when he'd stayed in her room and slept in her bed, right beside her...He hadn't just been saying the words he thought she wanted to hear, had he? A fresh wave of despair washed over Cassy and her sobs returned full-force.

"If he touched one hair on your head—" Papa growled.

"Now don't fly into a rage. Remember who he is."

"He's a debauched baron who will be a debauched duke, I know. But the core of a man does not change, Annabelle. If you think he has honorable intentions toward our daughter, you're as delusional as she is with all this ghost nonsense."

"It's not nonsense!" Cassy screamed. "There *is* a man in black and he's been following me. I can see him. He *is* real, Papa."

"Just like you saw my father after he was already dead and buried?" Papa spat, and the room fell instantly silent.

No one had mentioned that particular incident since Cassy was nine. In fact, Papa had forbidden her from ever speaking of it. It was so long ago, like a distant memory that she'd been certain she'd dreamed the whole thing. But what if she really had seen Grandpapa all those years ago? Papa had insisted that since she'd loved and missed Grandpapa so much it was natural to imagine he was still alive. But Cassy had been adamant that she hadn't imagined it, and she would have continued vowing that for the rest of her life if Papa hadn't slapped her for lying.

But Grandpapa *had* sat beside her on the edge of her bed. He'd told her not to be sad and made Cassy promise to be a good girl. The memory washed back over her. "I *did* see him," she breathed out for the first time in a decade, even if everyone else thought she was mad, even if Papa had forbade her from ever saying those words aloud.

"Oh for God's sake," Papa complained.

And then the air turned cold and Cassy could see her breath and then...and then the angry man in black appeared beside the wardrobe. He glared at her and the menacing look in his eyes terrified her. Cassy screamed, she couldn't help it.

～

*H*is ear pressed to the door, Jack winced slightly. Had Cassy seen her grandfather's ghost? Was that what they'd said? It was not terribly easy to overhear everything going on in her room.

And then a blood-curdling scream sounded through the

door and rattled the teeth in Jack's head. What the devil was going on in there?

"That's it!" Lady Widcombe announced. "Where is that doctor with the laudanum?"

Laudanum? Cassy wasn't ill, just…Well, she might be insane. But laudanum didn't cure that particular affliction. If it did, Lady Brauning would have recovered from her madness a decade ago.

The door handle jiggled and Jack bolted from his eavesdropping spot, around the closest corner.

A moment later, Cassy's cries seemed louder as though someone had, in fact, opened her door, and then she sounded muted once more. Dear God, what was he even doing standing there?

"Oh!" Lady Widcombe rounded the same corner and almost collided right into Jack. "Lord St. Giles, you nearly frightened me."

"My apologies," he muttered. "I hope Lady Cassandra is feeling better."

"How kind of you to ask." The countess' face brightened slightly. Most likely because Jack would be a duke someday, even if he was only a debauched baron at the moment. "She's not feeling well, I'm afraid. Though I'm sure she'll be much more herself tomorrow."

Which Cassy would that be? The kind girl Jack had fallen in love with? Or the frightened one who might very well be insane? "Would you please tell her that Oscar has been located? One of Keyvnor's neighbors found the poor little fellow."

Lady Widcombe's brow scrunched up. "I didn't realize Oscar was missing."

"Covered in mud, I'm afraid," Jack told her. "One of Banfield's maids is cleaning him now."

"Oh." The countess nodded. "Well, thank you very much,

Lord St. Giles. Now, if you'll please excuse me. I must find out what is keeping Doctor Fairfax."

"Of course, my lady," he replied as the countess hastened her pace down the corridor.

A moment later, Cassy wailed, "Don't let him touch me!"

Jack winced and raked a hand through his hair. This certainly was not the outcome he'd expected when he invited himself to Castle Keyvnor. He couldn't stand there all night and listen to her cry. Doing so would probably kill him. What he needed was a nice bottle of whisky he could crawl into. He was fairly certain he remembered seeing a bottle in the billiards room.

He made his way down to the corridor and to the steps, happy not to have encountered anyone on his way to the billiards room, and even happier when he spotted the bottle of whisky right where he thought he'd seen it.

Jack splashed some whisky into a tumbler and started toward one of the leather chairs in the far corner. He could wile away the rest of the night here until he was too deep in his cups to give any thoughts to angry ghosts, lost poodles, or…a beautiful but most definitely insane girl. What a bloody awful day.

"What a bloody awful day," Michael grumbled from the threshold, startling Jack and almost making him slosh whisky onto his cravat.

"Where the devil have you been all day?" Jack stared at his friend.

But Michael, who was generally loquacious, seemed to clamp his lips closed. "Just a bit of family business."

"And it was bloody awful?"

"Who said that?" His friend looked nervous all of a sudden.

"*You* did." Jack sat up straighter in his chair. "When you came in, you said 'what a bloody awful day.'" Which had been the exact same sentiment Jack had thought at the exact same moment.

"Just long, I meant." Michael stepped further into the room. "Thought there was a bottle of whisky in here the other day."

"Way ahead of you." Jack gestured to the sideboard along the far wall.

Michael crossed the floor and then splashed some whisky into a tumbler of his own. "Why aren't you at dinner with the others?" he asked as he made his way across the room to drop into the chair opposite Jack.

"Don't feel like being social this evening."

Michael smirked. "And here I'd gotten the feeling that you'd use any excuse to be near Cassy."

Rather than respond to that, Jack took a swallow from his drink. As the whisky burned its way down his throat, he leaned back against the chair and closed his eyes.

"My father blistered my ears over you today, by the way."

Jack opened his eyes again to judge if his friend was teasing him, but Michael looked more than serious, which was not a look he generally sported. "I haven't even done anything." At least nothing anyone knew anything about.

"You've made your interest in my cousin quite known. Uncle Peter tore into father and then father tore into me. So thank you for that."

"Widcombe is an ass," Jack replied. *He's a debauched baron who will be a debauched duke. But the core of a man does not change.* "He'd get along famously with my father."

"No one gets along with your father."

A ghost of a smile tugged on Jack's lips at the truth of Michael's words. "Aye, but they could bond over their shared disdain for me. Think how much fun they could have together."

Michael leaned back against his chair. "Honestly, Uncle

93

Peter wouldn't think a thing about you if you weren't chasing Cassy's skirts."

Jack blew out a breath. "No reason to give me another thought, then."

"What's that supposed to mean?"

It meant that no matter how much Jack had wanted a different outcome from this little journey, he was a man of reason. He had to be, no matter how much it pained him. "I don't believe we'll suit, after all."

Michael's mouth dropped open. "Are you mad?"

At that, a slightly mad sounding laugh *did* escape Jack. "That is the question, isn't it?"

Michael shook his head. "I'll admit, I didn't notice your attraction to her before. I'm not sure how I missed it, but—"

"I didn't want you to see it." Jack blew out a breath. "I'm not blind, Michael. I've seen the way you and Redgrave hover over Charlotte. I didn't need you doing the same with Cassy…er…Lady Cassandra."

The strangest expression settled on Michael's face. "Sometimes hovering is necessary to keep someone you love safe. And sometimes you have to do things you'd never imagined to accomplish the same goal."

Well, that was fairly enigmatic of him, which again wasn't like Michael in the least. "You're not yourself."

"I may never be again." He took a sip from his glass.

Was that all he intended to say? Jack frowned. "Well, would you like to share the reason?"

But Michael shook his head. "You'd never believe me anyway. Besides, we were talking about your sudden lack of interest in Cassy, which makes no sense at all, I have to say. I didn't see it before, Jack, but I've seen it since we arrived. You're different around her, you're—"

"In love with her," Jack supplied. "I am very aware of the

fact, Michael. But that doesn't change the fact that we will not suit."

His friend simply gaped at him, as though *Jack* was the one who was mad.

Jack scrubbed a hand down his face. Michael was Cassy's cousin, but he'd been Jack's friend for more than a dozen years. One of the best ones he'd ever had. And he needed to talk to someone, unburden his heart a little. "I don't think she's entirely sane."

"Cassandra Priske?" Michael frowned. "She's a million times more levelheaded than my sister."

Jack had thought so too, and one of the kindest girls he'd ever met, but... "Perhaps one can be both levelheaded and mad at the same time." He shook his head as that sentence sounded quite ridiculous to his own ears. "In the last two days, she has nearly come apart twice. Screaming and vowing that a ghostly man in black is chasing after her."

Michael didn't even gasp. Instead, he seemed to steel himself in his chair. "Did she say who he was? Lord Tyrrell or someone else?"

"What?"

"Did she say who he was?" Michael repeated.

"Uh, no," Jack returned slowly. "We forewent introductions."

"You should take her to the gypsy camp tomorrow. Or right this moment, even. Vail's grandmother can give her some kind of pouch to put in her bosom to keep her safe."

A pouch to put in her bosom? Jack's mouth fell open. "Do you even hear yourself?"

Michael nodded solemnly. "Yes, and I won't take back a word."

"And I thought it was the *De Lisle* side of the family that was mad."

"Just because you can't see something doesn't mean it's not there, Jack. Especially at Keyvnor."

CHAPTER 13

*C*assy couldn't even lift her head from her pillow. She didn't have the strength to move even one muscle. Must be the laudanum Doctor Fairfax had given her. Or probably the second dose Mama had forced down her throat after the doctor had left.

A couple of candles flickered across the room, making shadows dance along her walls, but Cassy couldn't even turn her head to see them.

"Are you dead?" A little boy's face appeared in her line of sight. He had light hair and almost translucent skin.

"I don't think so," she muttered, her voice sounding hoarse to her own ears.

"You're pretty." He smiled and reached his hand out as though to stroke her cheek, but his touch felt like a cool wind against her skin.

Heavens! Was he a figment of her imagination? Or another of Keyvnor's ghosts? "Who are you?"

"Paul Hambly," he said softly.

"Paul Hambly?" The late Earl of Banfield's son? His *dead* son?

He nodded, his smile brightening. "Who are you?"

"Are *you* dead?" she echoed his earlier question.

The boy's smile vanished. "I think so." Then he nodded again. "I've been here a long time."

Four or five decades. He was her father's cousin. Or had been when he was alive. If she wasn't imagining all of this. Was she really talking to a ghost child? Or was the laudanum playing tricks with her mind. "Are you real?"

He nodded.

"Am I the only one who can see you?" She was, after all, the only one who seemed able to see the angry man dressed in black.

Paul shook his head. "I've talked to others before." And then his eyes went wide and he backed away from her bed. "Someone's here. I have to go." Then he vanished in the blink of an eye.

"Paul!" she called just as her door opened and Betsy stepped into her room.

"Lady Widcombe asked me to sit with you tonight, Lady Cassandra," her maid said as Oscar hopped up onto the bed, padded across the counterpane and dropped his chin on Cassy's belly.

At least with Betsy and Oscar she wouldn't be alone. "Thank you," she croaked out. "Did Lord St. Giles find Oscar?"

Betsy settled into a chair beside Cassy's bed. "No, a neighbor. A Mr. Cardew I think Mrs. Bray said."

Had Jack even looked for Oscar like he'd promised? Or had Mr. Cardew simply had better luck? "So glad someone found him."

"Poor boy was covered in mud," Betsy said. "But he's had a bath and is perfectly clean now." Then she shivered slightly. "It is cold in here, isn't it?"

If Cassy could have nodded, she would have. "I think there's a blanket at the edge of the bed."

"Aye, my lady." As Betsy retrieved the blanket, she looked directly at Oscar and said, "If Mrs. Bray catches you on the bed, we'll both be done for."

Oscar barked in agreement.

"He'll hop down if she comes in here," Cassy promised, happy to have her poodle by her side.

The comfort of Oscar was the first bit of peace she'd felt since Jack had handed her off to Papa. Had he really decided she was mad? Had he been relieved to turn her over to Papa and wash his hands of her? Tears pooled in her eyes, which she hadn't known was possible. She'd cried so much today, she wasn't certain how she had any tears left.

"The laudanum has made me groggy, Betsy." She closed her eyes and hoped doing so would keep her from crying. "Tell me something, anything, 'til I fall asleep." Anything that wouldn't make her think about Jack or about that fact that he hadn't even thought to check on her. Anything that wouldn't make her heart hurt anymore than it already did.

Dutifully, Betsy began relaying one bit of staff gossip after another until Cassy's eyes lids were too heavy to open.

❧

*T*he bit of sun there was to be found in Cornwall poured into the sitting room, and Jack tried for the millionth time that day to read the first sentence of the Times article he'd started sometime after breakfast. But if he hadn't tasted anything he ate that morning, he also couldn't be pressed upon to relay that first sentence.

It had been a bloody awful, restless night. He was fairly certain he didn't get as much as even one wink of sleep. How could he when every time he closed his eyes he saw Cassy's face? The whole thing was making him bloody insane, right along with her.

And even though he knew, logically, that he should keep his distance, leave Keyvnor the next morning, in fact, he'd still found himself pacing the corridor in front of Cassy's room in the middle of the night, warring with himself whether or not he should enter. In his weakest moment, when he finally had pushed her door open, he'd spotted a slight little maid snoring away in a chair beside her bed. He'd quickly retreated after that, but he still hadn't slept.

Though he supposed when the life he had mapped out for himself had completely unraveled, sleeping would be near impossible.

From the threshold, he heard a number of sudden hisses as though a pit of vipers had taken up residence in the corridor outside the sitting room. Jack glanced in the general direction to find Michael, Redgrave and Lady Charlotte standing just barely on the other side of the doorway looking at him as though he was some foreign specimen.

"*He* is not the one." Michael grumbled, loud enough for Jack to hear.

What the devil now? And why were they looking at him like that? "Which one?" he asked, pushing out of his chair and dropping the paper into his vacant spot.

"Never mind them," Lady Charlotte said as she breezed past her brothers into the sitting room. "Would you care to stroll with me?"

Not particularly. He was in a rotten mood and would rather not subject Lady Charlotte to his sourness if it could be helped, but what other choice did he have? Refusing her request would be the height of rudeness.

Her lashes fluttered coquettishly and Jack was fairly certain his eyes rounded in surprise as trepidation settled in his gut. What the devil? Was she trying to *flirt* with him? And with her brothers standing watch from the threshold? Was this some sort of trick? Something Redgrave had devised so he could call Jack out or something of the like?

"Just for a moment." Lady Charlotte blinked up at him, a soft smile gracing her lips. "This won't take long."

Before Jack could respond, she linked her arm with his and practically dragged him into the corridor past her brothers. He glanced back at Michael, hoping for a bit of assistance.

"Go!" Michael and Redgrave both ordered in unison.

So it wasn't only the DeLisles' side of the family that was mad, apparently. That fact had become abundantly clear over the last day. He glared at his traitorous friend as Lady Charlotte began to lead him down the corridor.

"So tell me," she began, "are you still charming maids and dogs?"

He couldn't possibly have heard her correctly. "Lady Charlotte?"

But she wasn't looking at Jack. She was peering into her left hand, looking at...an *emerald*? Was that really what she was doing? Yes, the Becks' and Priske's side of the family was just as mad as the DeLisles' side. There was no question about that.

"Dogs and maids," Lady Charlotte repeated.

His patience long since gone, Jack heaved an irritable sigh. "What exactly is this about, my lady?"

"Nothing, my lord." She heaved a sigh of her own and glanced back up at him. "I am sorry to have bothered you." Then she dropped his arm and started back toward the sitting room and her awaiting brothers.

Jack watched her departing form and frowned. Something was going on with that trio. Something very odd. Michael Beck was going to owe him an answer or two, but not apparently now as the three siblings all departed in a rush for who knew where else. All Jack could do was stare after them in confusion.

Actually, the whole interaction with Lady Charlotte was troubling on a number of levels. Not only had the entire thing made absolutely no sense, but Jack hadn't felt any kind of reaction to the lady. No matter the coquettish batting of her lashes or her attempt at a seductive smile, nothing had stirred within his blood. Perhaps it was because the chit was Michael's sister, and her brothers were not far away; but she *was* a very pretty lady. He'd normally feel *something* if a woman was attempting a flirtation. But he suspected, deep in his heart, that he would never feel anything – not longing, lust or otherwise – for any other lady in the world for the rest of his days. Cassy had completely ruined him in that regard, it seemed.

He'd been so worried about what his life would be like *with* her, madness and all; but what would his life be like with*out* her now? Now that he knew what it felt like to hold her in his arms? Now that his every waking thought was of her? Now that he knew he loved her?

Meaningless.

His life would be meaningless without her. Jack knew that in the pit of his stomach. He was damned if he did, damned if he didn't. There was no way of getting around that.

A little black ball of fluff raced to where Jack stood and dropped in front of his feet, thumping his tail against the runner and panting up at Jack expectantly. "Glad to see you're not lost *today*, Oscar," he muttered.

"Oscar!" Cassy's voice drifted around the corner and the lyrical sound brought Jack to full attention.

And a moment later, *she* rounded the corner, looking as beautiful as ever and not resembling the mad lady he'd handed over to her father the day before in the least.

"Oh!" Her hand fluttered to her heart before her gaze dropped to the floor. "My lord."

Jack's heart twisted more than a bit. Was that who he was to her now? Lord St. Giles again? "My lady," he followed her rather formal lead. "I hope you're doing well."

"Thank you," she replied, still not looking at him. Then she slapped a hand to her leg. "Come on, Oscar. Time to go."

The poodle looked from Cassy back to Jack as though he didn't want to leave without being rewarded. Jack bit back a smile. "No treats today, I'm afraid, pup."

"Oscar!" Cassy said sharply.

Jack should let her leave. He should be relieved that she seemed inclined to do so. But watching her start back around that corner tore at his heart. "Cassy, wait," he called out.

～

*C*assy didn't move an inch, even though she wanted to run back to her borrowed chambers, throw herself upon her four poster and cry her eyes out. Papa had been right about him. She'd seen that flash of judgment in Jack's eyes when she'd come upon him a moment earlier. He *did* think she was mad, and that hurt like nothing else ever had. "Yes?" she replied over her shoulder, relieved her voice hadn't cracked.

"You won't even look at me?" he asked. "Have I done something to upset you, my lady?"

He'd only hurt her to her core. Of course Cassy didn't want to look at him. She didn't want to see that judgmental expression in his eyes again. It was like a dagger to her heart. "Do you believe me? About the man in black?"

He blew out a breath. "I have never laid eyes on the fellow."

"That didn't answer my question, Lord St. Giles. Do you

believe me or not? The other night you said you did, but I suspect you weren't being honest with me then."

Jack came up behind her, so close the heat from his body warmed her back. "I believe *you* believe it."

Well, of course, *she* believed it. She couldn't help the snort that escaped her. "I'm so relieved you don't think I've invented him to garner attention."

"How many of these apparitions have you seen? Your grandfather? The man in black? How many others?"

Cassy gasped at the mention of her grandfather and spun on her heel to face him then. "How do you know about my grandfather?"

Jack shrugged. "How many others have you seen?"

She was not about to answer that, not until he answered her. "*How* do you know about my grandfather? No one knows about that."

He heaved a sigh. "I came to your chambers yesterday and overheard you and your parents."

He'd come to her chambers? Heavens! "Did anyone see you?"

He shook his head. "Your mother bumped into me, but she seems much more enthralled with my future dukedom than anything else."

Cassy's face heated. How awful that he'd overheard her parents yesterday. Mama had been particularly vulgar with her status seeking. Somehow that was much more embarrassing than Jack thinking she was insane.

"How many ghosts *have* you seen?"

More than she wanted to admit to him. "What does it matter? You won't believe me." And she didn't want to see that disbelief flash in his silvery eyes again. It was painful enough the first time.

"I've been *with* you, Cassy. The other night after whist and yesterday in the maze. There was no man in black. I would have seen him if he was there."

"Not necessarily." After all, Samantha hadn't seen Grandpapa when he'd come to the nursery all those years ago.

A muscle ticked in Jack's jaw as though that particular response wasn't one he appreciated. "I need to know if you're entirely sane."

And the fact that he thought she wasn't felt like someone had slugged her. "You've already decided I'm not." She heaved a sigh. "Nothing I could say one way or the other would change your mind about that."

Oscar barked in agreement. At least she still had Oscar.

"I won't hold you to any declarations from the other evening," Cassy added. Then she turned back on her heel and continued down the corridor with Oscar at her side.

CHAPTER 14

*I*n hindsight, Jack probably should have left Keyvnor first thing that morning or at least after his encounter with Cassy that afternoon. He should have hopped in his coach and started for Kent or...really anywhere else. He shouldn't be sitting at dinner, torturing himself as he watched Cassy from the other end of the table. And he definitely shouldn't have questioned her about her sanity that afternoon. He doubted she'd ever look in his direction or speak to him again. Hindsight.

If he could take back the words he'd said, he'd do so in a heartbeat. Nothing had changed from that conversation. He already knew she'd seen ghosts or apparitions or figments of her imagination, or whatever the devil it was she saw. What did it matter if she'd seen one, two or a hundred? Either he could accept that she had seen, or thought she had seen, something; or he couldn't. The number of her sightings meant very little in the grand scheme of things.

"Are you headed to Vail's gypsy wedding tomorrow?" Chadwick Kendall asked, as he speared a carrot with his fork.

Jack hadn't uttered one word to the fellow beside him all night. In his distracted state, he was an abysmal conversationalist. "I beg your pardon?"

"Vail's gypsy wedding tomorrow. Are you planning on attending?" Kendall asked again.

Damn it all. Adam Vail was getting *married*? The man hadn't mentioned anything of the sort when Jack had seen him a few days ago. Even if he had, attending a wedding right now would hardly be high on the list of things Jack wanted to do. "After attending a gypsy funeral earlier this week, I think I've had my fill of the lot." Besides a wedding, gypsy or otherwise, would only make him think about Cassy and about how close he'd come to having his dreams of her realized.

"You've taken an interest in Lady Cassandra, have you not?" Kendall glanced down the table in the direction Jack had stared all evening.

At this point, it was far from a secret. Jack snorted. "I hardly see why that's any of your concern."

Kendall shrugged. "Just curious what you thought about the family."

Jack thought Lady Widcombe was a social climbing harpy and that Lord Widcombe was an overbearing arse. But he didn't know Kendall well enough to say either of those things. "Like anyone else, I suppose." He did like Cassy's little brother, however. So he added, "Though, Toby Priske reminds me of me at his age."

"Really?" Kendall's brow lifted in surprise.

"Loves tormenting his sisters. I did convince him to leave them alone the first day they arrived."

Kendall chuckled. "How did you manage that?"

Jack shrugged. "Told him his skills were better suited for causing havoc for any *fellow* chasing after his sisters, instead. It was his duty to keep them safe, and all that."

"You weren't worried about him causing havoc for you?"

At that, Jack couldn't help but smile. "I'm the one who gave him the idea. He trusts *me*. Though I would hate to be any other fellow chasing after a Priske sister."

Kendall seemed to swallow a bit uneasily at that.

And Jack's stomach churned slightly. Did the fellow have his eye on Cassy too? As Chadwick Kendall was not heir to the Margate dukedom, he wouldn't have any luck getting Lady Widcombe's approval.

Kendall returned his attention to his plate and Jack's returned to Cassy once more. She was so beautiful it almost hurt to look at her. He knew the exact feel of her pretty porcelain skin, the lilac scent of her raven hair that was pulled back in a loose chignon, the taste of her lips which were currently pressed against a goblet.

Damn it all. He'd made a giant mess of things. He'd come so close to having exactly what he wanted...Even the worry over her potential madness couldn't extinguish the love and admiration he'd felt for her since that night so long ago at Vauxhall. Was that what Brauning felt for his wife? That he'd suffer through life with a mad woman, because not having that woman would drive him mad instead?

Shortly after the ladies left the men to their port, Jack excused himself and made his way to the drawing room, hoping for another word, another chance to put things to back to rights with Cassy...

...But she wasn't there.

Her mother did smile at him from across the room and wave her fingers in the air. Jack gritted his teeth through a false smile. No reason to turn the countess against him. After all, she might just be the only Priske who approved of him at the moment, even if the reason for that approval had nothing to do with him and everything to do with his father's title.

He moved on quickly, not wanting to get drawn into a

conversation with anyone if he could help it. The only person in the world he wanted to talk to was Cassy. Perhaps she'd already retired to her chambers. Jack did know where that was, so he made his way directly there...or would have, if he hadn't spotted her maid enter her chambers a moment before.

Jack blew out a breath in frustration. Exactly how long would he have to wait for her servant to leave? Was the girl planning on staying with her all night again? How would he get a chance to speak with her if that was the case? There was nothing to do but wait, at least until he devised a plan to deal with Cassy's maid.

"St. Giles!" came Toby's exuberant voice from behind Jack.

He glanced over his shoulder at Cassy's little brother and nodded. He wasn't the Priske Jack wanted to speak with, but he would do. He could be just the fellow to help distract Cassy's maid for a bit. "Toby! I trust you've had an uneventful day at Keyvnor."

The boy grinned. "A little eventful," he admitted. "I am glad you told me to keep an eye on my sisters."

"Oh?"

Toby nodded. "I've got my eye on one fellow here, a black-hearted scoundrel, I'm sure."

Good God. Was he on to Jack, after all? How unfortunate. "Indeed?" He turned fully to face the boy.

"I don't like the way that Mr. Kendall has been looking at Samantha."

Kendall and Lady Samantha! That explained the look on Kendall's face at dinner. Jack nearly laughed! The man probably wanted to call him out about now, especially if Toby had turned his tormenting focus on the fellow. "Chasing her skirts, is he?"

"Nothing I can't handle," Toby replied.

And Jack had no doubt the boy was correct on that front. He probably should feel sorry for Kendall, but he was much more concerned about Toby's oldest sister. "I was keeping an eye on Lady Cassandra, but she didn't look well at dinner. I don't suppose you'd mind checking on her in her chambers? Letting her know I was asking about her?"

The grin on Toby's face spread even further. "Cassy's not in her chambers. She's outside."

She was? "Are you sure?"

Toby chuckled. "If you're keeping your eye on her, St. Giles, you're not doing a very good job of it. Saw her go out through the south doors just a few minutes ago."

The south doors. Perfect. "Well, I'll just check on her myself outside, then."

A flash of something sparked in Toby's eyes. "Are you chasing after *Cassy's* skirts?"

"You're not going to splash ink in my tea, are you?"

Toby shook his head. "You're the one fellow in England who would be on to me if I tried that."

Jack supposed that was true. But who knew what else Toby Priske might come up with on his own? Who knew what he'd done to Chadwick Kendall over the last few days? "If it makes you feel any better, I'm *not* chasing Cassy's skirts. I love her. I want to marry her, just as soon as possible."

The boy regarded Jack with a suspicious eye. "My father doesn't like you at all, you know?"

That Jack was well aware of. "Well, it's a good thing I don't want to marry him, then, isn't it?"

"It is." A laugh escaped Toby. "But I don't think he'd accept an offer from you for Cassy."

Jack suspected the boy was correct on that front. Widcombe did not sound undecided about Jack at all. *He's a debauched baron who will be a debauched duke. The core of a man does not change.*

Widcombe's words echoed in Jack's ears once more. "At the moment, I'm only concerned with whether or not your sister would accept my offer. She's outside through the south doors?"

Toby nodded. "If she refuses you, though, just fair warning about watching your tea."

Jack bit back a smile. Toby Priske *was* just like Jack had been at his age. "I'll consider myself warned."

~

*C*harlotte was getting married tomorrow. Cassy hadn't believed it when her cousin had informed her of the fact late that afternoon, and she still couldn't believe it. The whole thing seemed very surreal. The very last thing in the world she expected when she'd been forced to Keyvnor was that she'd attend her cousin's wedding while she was there. Charlotte hadn't even known Mr. Vail before they'd arrived in Cornwall. And tomorrow she'd marry the man….who was half-gypsy? How did such a thing like that even happen so quickly?

She continued down the little path, heading toward the sea, which Cassy could faintly hear in the distance. The sound of the waves crashing against the shore was much more soothing than sitting inside the castle and waiting for one ghost or another to show themselves to her.

Thankfully the moon was full in the sky above her and lit the path at her feet. The sound of the waves got louder and louder, and Cassy was tempted never to return to Keyvnor. She'd rather stay out all night and watch the sunrise in the morning than sleep in her borrowed chambers another evening. The only night that had been pleasant at the castle had been the night Jack had stayed with her…But he'd never stay with her again. He'd never hold her again. He'd never kiss her again. He thought she was mad as a March hare. That much was very clear.

While Charlotte would marry her half-gypsy Mr. Vail tomorrow, Cassy would live the rest of her life without Jack. Her heart twisted at the truth of that thought, but it was true. She knew it was. She'd stupidly fallen in love with the dashing rake when she'd known all along that she should keep her distance from him. The thought of his lies made her heart ache and a lump form in her throat. She'd so foolishly believed him. She'd so foolishly fallen for him. And she *was* a fool. There was no doubt about that.

"Cassy!" she heard in the distance, or thought she did.

Cassy glanced over her shoulder toward the castle and *did* see the shape of man rushing in her direction. She stood rooted to the ground and focused on the figure until she recognized him...Jack.

What in the world did he want with her now? To question her further about ghosts and shadowy men? To try to explain why he'd been less than honest with her? To stare at her like she was a Bedlamite as he'd done all through dinner?

"Go away, Jack!" she called back.

Of course he didn't. Of course he kept walking right for her. Because Jack Hazelwood always did what he wanted without regard to anyone else's thoughts on the matter.

She punched her hands to her hips and glared at him as he reached her. "I have nothing to say to you."

"I have so much to say to you," he replied softly and reached his hand out to her. "Please don't turn me away, Cassy."

She glanced down at his outstretched hand, her heart pounding in her chest. What *did* he want with her? Then she glanced back up to meet his silvery eyes, which held hers with the sincerity she saw in his depths. The moonlight reflected off his dark hair and her breath caught in her throat. "What is it, Jack?"

"I love you," he said simply.

And she loved him too, even if she didn't want to. "You think I'm insane."

"Perhaps." He didn't even flinch. "Or perhaps not, I'm not entirely certain."

For a man who was known for his charming nature, that was hardly a pleasant thing to say. "I don't think we have anything else to talk about, Jack."

She turned to continue on the path toward the ocean, but Jack caught her arm in his grasp. He was so close to her back, the heat of him warmed her through the silk of her gown. "I *do* know that I'll go mad myself if you walk away from me," he rumbled near her ear.

Cassy glanced over her shoulder to meet his gaze once more.

"Tell me you love me too, Cassy. Tell me we can find a way to make this work, because I don't want to lose you."

Heavens. Was he serious? Her foolish heart lifted just a bit. "What way, Jack? You think I'm mad and that hurts worse than anything."

He heaved a sigh. "I haven't seen any man in black, Cassy. I haven't. I don't know what you've seen, if anything. I only know what I've seen with my own eyes. You can't fault me for that."

"You told me I was levelheaded, that you believed me." Cassy heaved a sigh of her own.

"I *did*," he stressed. "But then you collapsed in the maze in the middle of the day when I was right there, and I heard your parents talking about your grandfather, all of it was very worrisome."

Tears began to well up in her eyes.

"But I love you anyway, Cassy. Isn't it possible you can

love me even if I don't see the same things you do? Isn't the fact that we love each other more important than that?"

She hadn't thought of it that way. Even her own parents didn't believe her. Was it fair to be angry at Jack because he didn't? She wished he could believe her, but if he couldn't…If he could accept her *despite* that fact, didn't that count for something?

"Say *something*, love," he urged. "Toby's already told me if you won't marry me, I'll have to look for ink in my tea from here on out."

She couldn't help the laugh that escaped her. That would only serve him right after the guidance he'd given her brother. "You have no one to blame for that except yourself."

"Save me from myself, then." His smile made her belly flip. "Marry me, Cassy. Please say you will?"

He wanted to marry her? He *still* wanted to marry her? She spun on her heel and threw her arms around his neck. Jack's hands settled at her waist, nearly singeing her with his touch.

He held her close and kissed the side of her cheek. "Is that a yes?"

She nodded quickly. "Yes, yes, yes!"

And then he captured her lips with a kiss that most definitely branded her as his. Jack's fingers clutched her tighter to him and his tongue slipped inside her mouth, making her knees weak. If she wasn't holding him tight, she'd have collapsed to the path at his feet. She breathed in the sandalwood scent of him and kissed him back just as fiercely.

After a lifetime had passed, Jack lifted his head and smiled down at her. Cassy could almost float up to the clouds.

"Shall we make a run for Scotland?" he asked, his silvery eyes twinkling just slightly.

Scotland! They were in the furthest corner in England from Scotland. She shook her head. "Are you mad?"

His brow lifted in jest. That probably was a poor choice of words, considering he thought it likely *she* was mad. "I don't have any confidence that your father will accept my suit, Cassy."

Papa did not care for Jack in the least. He was right about that. "But Scotland? Papa would find us long before we reached the border."

"We can hire a vessel in the village to sail us there. We could gain a substantial lead if we leave right away."

Sail to Scotland? That was tempting and wildly romantic. Still… "Charlotte is getting married tomorrow. She'd never forgive me if I missed the event."

Jack blinked at her. "Lady *Charlotte* is marrying Adam Vail?"

Cassy nodded. "I was more than surprised when she told me as much this afternoon. I don't think she's known him long at all."

A smile lit Jack's lips. "Sometimes it just takes a chance meeting or a glance across the south walk at Vauxhall to alter your life forever."

She supposed that was true. Cassy bit her bottom lip before suggesting, "We could hire a vessel in the village after the wedding."

"Perfect suggestion." Jack lowered his head and kissed her once more.

CHAPTER 15

*H*is last night at Castle Keyvnor and Jack was not about to spend it alone. Tomorrow he and Cassy would hop a ship for Scotland and tonight they'd spend their last evening in Cornwall wrapped in each other's arms. He waited in the corridor outside her chambers until after her meek little maid had departed and then he slipped inside Cassy's room.

She was stunning in her pink wrapper, but Jack wanted nothing more than to tug on her sash and divest her of every strip she was wearing.

Oscar barked in greeting and thumped his tail against the counterpane, drawing Jack's attention from Cassy's vision in pink to her poodle. He smiled at the dog. It was a good thing the little fellow liked him since they'd be with each other from here on out. "I suppose he'll have his fill of fish by the time we reach Scotland."

"You'll spoil him rotten." Cassy crossed the room and slid her hands up his chest to settle at the nape of his neck, trailing want and need everywhere she touched him.

Jack dipped his head down to hers and replied across her lips, "It's you I want to spoil," before kissing her once again.

She sighed against his lips and Jack pulled on her sash until her wrapper fell open, and then he slid the soft muslin from her arms to let it fall at their feet. He pulled back slightly to gaze down at her as he fingered the lacy bodice of her nightrail. "I cannot wait for you to be my wife."

"I can't wait either." An endearing blush stained her cheeks, which only made him want her even more.

Jack shrugged out of his jacket and jerked at his cravat. They were starting for Scotland tomorrow, why torture himself the entire sailing? They would be man and wife soon enough. "Then let's not wait."

He scooped Cassy up in his arms, which elicited a surprised giggle from her. "Jack!"

Her warm hazel eyes sparkled just so and Jack couldn't help but laugh right along with her. She was delightful, utterly delightful in everyway. Life with Cassy would be everything he'd ever wanted and more. He placed her gently in the middle of the four-poster and then quickly dispensed with his waistcoat.

She watched him eagerly, which made Jack yank his shirt over his head and start on the fastenings of his trousers.

Cassy slid up the bed, closer to the pillows and looked slightly nervous for the first time.

"Nothing to worry about, love," he said softly. Then he dropped onto the edge of the bed and tugged at his Hessians. Oscar padded across the counterpane and laid his head next to Jack's leg. The little poodle was going to need to make himself scarce in a moment.

~

117

*N*othing to worry about. Easy for him to say. Cassy took a staggering breath, praying she wasn't a fool. Without marriage, Jack could ruin her if he was of a mind after tonight; but if her father caught up to them before they made it to Scotland, he would be much more likely to let her continue on with Jack if their relationship had been consummated. Jack hadn't said those words, and he might not be even thinking them, but she was. Papa hated Jack. He would never allow her to marry him, unless...Well, unless he didn't have a choice.

She believed Jack loved her. She could see the truth of that shining in his eyes whenever he looked at her. And she certainly loved him. So she shouldn't really be nervous, should she?

"What's wrong, Cassy?" Jack asked as his boots dropped to the rug.

"I love you," she said quietly.

The rakish smile that spread across his face made heat pool deep within her. "I am relieved to hear it." Then he gently nudged Oscar off the side of the bed. "Sorry, boy, not going to share her with you tonight."

"Poor Oscar." A nervous laugh escaped Cassy.

"Poor Oscar?" Jack scoffed as he shifted on the bed and loomed over her. "Poor Jack," he teased. "He's had you all to himself while I've been pining for you more than a year."

She couldn't help but smile at that. "Poor Jack."

"That's better." He leaned forward and brushed his lips against hers.

The anxiety that had taken hold of her began to evaporate, and was completely forgotten when Jack's fingers caressed one of her breasts, tracing a circle around her nipple which strained against the muslin of her nightrail.

"Jack," she breathed out as frissons of need danced across her skin.

"You're so beautiful," he said reverently. Then he tugged her bodice lower until her breasts popped free. Jack dipped his head and captured one nipple with his mouth while his fingers teased the other, lightly pinching and twisting her until Cassy bucked beneath him.

Breathless, heat pulsed in her core. Then Jack's hand trailed down her belly to settle against her springy curls, and...Heavens! She'd never experienced anything so wonderfully amazing as when he touched her *there*.

She sucked in a surprised breath, and Jack chuckled against her breast. And then...Then one of his fingers pressed inside her and Cassy couldn't help the moan that escaped her.

Jack pinched her nipple and sucked the other into his mouth while his finger continued to work in and out of her. Cassy was fairly certain she'd splinter in two, but then he slid his finger from her warmth and pushed up on his arms, staring down at her with a hungry expression she'd never seen before.

He was so breathtakingly handsome. The twinkle in his silvery eyes, the dimple in his chin, the rakish smile that graced his lips. Her gaze drifted lower to his bare chest that she'd only felt, but had never seen until now. "I love you, Cassy," he said, bringing her gaze back to his eyes. "And I will see to your happiness every day of our lives."

Such a sweet vow. "And I will see to yours," she promised. She brushed her fingers against his chest, reveling in the feel of his strength beneath her fingertips.

He kneed her legs apart and Cassy caught the first glimpse of *him*, as Jack took himself in his hand, tugging slightly. Good heavens! He didn't mean to put that inside her, did he?

He did mean to. Cassy sucked in another breath as Jack's gaze locked with hers and he pressed himself against her slickness. And then he pushed the tip of himself inside her, stretching her around him. She gasped. And then he pushed even deeper. Heavens! There was nothing that felt like Jack possessing her, nothing in the world and she didn't want it to ever end.

Jack lowered his head, pressed his lips to hers, and then thrust fully inside her. A flash of pain wrenched through her and Cassy couldn't help but whimper.

"Sorry, love," Jack whispered across her lips. "It won't be like that again." And then he pulled back slightly from her and then thrust again. Oh! That was nice, the feel of him fully seated within her. And then he moved in and out, finding a rhythm that drove her wild, making a pressure build, and build, and then...

"Jack!" she called out as the first wave of release washed over her.

A moment later, a guttural groan escaped him and Jack collapsed atop her. He breathed heavily against her skin and Cassy wrapped her arms around him, loving the feel of the weight of him as though they were still joined as one.

Jack pressed a kiss to her breastbone and then rolled to her side and drew her into his arms. "Dear God, Cassy," he breathed out.

She kissed his chest and reveled in the feel of his arms around her and the hum of her body. "I love you."

"I love you," he whispered.

~

*J*ack woke with a start. Damn it all, had the bed shook beneath them? Or had it been a dream? Jack blinked into the darkness, but the chamber was dark as pitch and...freezing. How the devil had it gotten so cold? He reached for the counterpane to wrap around himself and Cassy, but it was stuck as though...Well, as though a poodle was hogging the whole thing for himself.

"Oscar," Jack grumbled under his breath. And the little dog *was* snoring near his feet.

His eyes slowly adjusted to the darkness and...Mother of God! He gasped and was certain his heart would pound out of his chest. Standing at the side of the bed, glaring at Cassy's sleeping form was a man, dressed in black. He looked like a sailor from the seventeenth century with his hat, baggy breeches and thigh-length coat.

A bit of fear tiptoed down his spine, and Jack tugged Cassy closer to him in an attempt to protect her, though he wasn't quite sure how to protect her from such a creature. The man in black, the sailor, shifted his gaze to Jack and the hatred in his black-as-night eyes stuck terror in his heart.

"Leave!" he ordered the ghost, or whatever it was.

"Jack?" Cassy mumbled. "What's wrong?"

The man reached his hand down toward Cassy, and Jack scrambled over top of her, blocking her from the sailor's reach. A coolness seemed to pierce right through him.

Cassy bolted upright in bed and sucked in a surprised breath. "Jack," she said cautiously. "Do you see—"

"I see him, love." And he did see him, as unbelievable as it seemed. "Get dressed. We're leaving Keyvnor."

"Now?" she whispered.

"Right now." He tossed his legs over the side of the bed, prepared to confront the sailor, or try to. But the man faded into the darkness as though he'd never been there. But he *had* been there. Jack had seen the thing with his very eyes.

There was no time to waste. They needed to leave the castle immediately and never return. Jack tossed his shirt back on and started for his trousers. But…Cassy hadn't moved an inch.

"I think he's gone, Cassy. We should go before he comes back."

"You *saw* him?" she asked again, a bit of emotion in her voice. "You really saw him this time?"

Jack hadn't even thought about the fact that Cassy wasn't mad, that there truly was some ghostly entity at Keyvnor, in her chambers. He sat on the edge of her bed and reached his hand out to her. "I will never doubt you again."

A genuine smile spread across her face and she threw her arms around his neck. He held her close, so relieved she was unharmed.

"Get dressed, love. We're not staying here one second longer than necessary."

She pulled back slightly. "Charlotte's wedding tomorrow?"

"We'll send our regards."

She grinned and his heart lightened a bit.

~

*W*ith just the clothes on their backs and Oscar trailing after them, Cassy and Jack slipped into the corridor. They wouldn't find a vessel in the middle of the night, she knew that; but they could head to the docks and wait for sunrise. Leaving Keyvnor felt like a weight had been lifted from her shoulders.

And Jack had seen the man in black. He *knew* Cassy wasn't mad. That was priceless. She knew he loved her either way, but now he knew and…that weight on her shoulders lifted even more.

Jack clutched her hand as though he never meant to let her go, and she was happy to never have him do so.

Oscar barked and Cassy winced. "Oscar!" she hissed. "Shhh!"

He barked again.

"Cassandra Priske!" Papa's voice echoed from somewhere behind them.

That weight on her shoulders came crashing back. She glanced up at Jack who tugged her hand, drawing her closer to him.

"Cassandra! Where do you think you're going?" Papa bellowed.

Jack turned on his heel, bringing Cassy with him. "We are leaving, Widcombe," he said crisply.

"The devil if you're going anywhere with my daughter."

Oh, heavens! Why did Papa have to stumble upon them now? Why had Oscar barked right outside her parents' door? Why couldn't they have made their escape before anyone awoke?

"You don't approve of me," Jack began. "I am well aware. But I love Cassy and she loves me, and we're not spending one more moment at Castle Keyvnor."

"She is *my* daughter, and I'll say where she goes and with whom."

"I'm marrying Jack, Papa," Cassy said, finding her voice.

"Over my dead body."

"Only if you force the issue," Jack returned coolly.

"Jack," Cassy whispered.

But he shook his head. "You can either give us your blessing or we'll leave without it, Widcombe. But either way, we will not be separated."

"Cassandra?" Mama poked her head out from their room. "What are you doing?" And then her eyes widened. "Lord St. Giles?"

"Congratulations, Lady Widcombe," Jack began, "your

daughter will be a duchess someday. Cassy and I will make certain to visit you on our way back from Scotland."

Oscar barked in agreement.

"Oh!" Mama's hand fluttered to her chest

Jack heaved a sigh, sank down to his haunches, and scooped Oscar up in his arms. "Come on, boy." Then he pushed back to his full height, squeezed Cassy's hand and started once more for the castle's main entrance – together, like they would spend the rest of their lives.

EPILOGUE

Village Church, Drummore Scotland ~ November 1811

There were no blacksmiths in the seaside village of Drummore, prepared to marry eloping Englishmen and their would-be brides over an anvil, which Cassy was certain would make her mother happy to learn at some point. There was, however, a very quaint chapel with a crusty, old vicar whom Jack had persuaded, with the help of a hefty sum, to perform the ceremony.

After a week aboard the Prickly Porpoise, Captain Jacobsen and his first mate had agreed to serve as Jack and Cassy's witnesses, also for a hefty sum. Though Jack didn't seem to mind. He just grinned from ear to ear and promised Cassy that the rest of their days would be grander than the last sennight had been. It would be difficult to be less grand than the Prickly Porpoise, but Cassy hadn't minded, not really. She had Jack and he had her, and any inconvenience in the short term mattered very little, not when they were going to be together the rest of their lives.

As Vicar McKittrick wasn't anxious for the Cornish

seamen, who were a rather odiferous pair, to stay terribly long inside his chapel, the ceremony was quite brief, probably just as speedy as any anvil wedding in Gretna Green would have been. Still, it was a church and Mama would be happy about that.

Their vows were quickly exchanged and after one brief kiss, the vicar declared them man and wife, and shooed them on their way.

Oscar was waiting outside the church doors, as Vicar McKittrick had drawn the line at Cornish fishermen *only* when it came to witnesses. When Cassy and Jack stepped back out into the sunlight, Oscar barked and scampered over to them. She bent down and scooped him up into her arms as Jack offered his thanks to Captain Jacobsen and his man.

"Will you need to sail back to Cornwall?" Jacobsen asked, pocketing the coins Jack had just given him.

But Jack shook his head. "We have no reason to ever return to Bocka Morrow or Castle Keyvnor." Then he glanced around at their sparse surroundings in Drummore and added, "Though, since you *are* headed south, perhaps you could take us as far as Liverpool?"

"Happily, milord," Jacobsen returned. He nodded for his first mate and the two of them started quickly back toward the docks.

Jack's hand landed on the small of Cassy's back and he sent her a smile that nearly made her melt. "Lady St. Giles, I propose we head for Cheshire."

"Cheshire?" Cassy had never been to Cheshire and Jack hadn't mentioned it until now.

He nodded, his silvery eyes twinkling just so. "Merrytree Cottage, near Ellesmere Port. Part of my mother's dowry. Haven't been there in nearly a decade, but I think you'd like it."

Heavens, she'd been so focused on making it to Scotland,

Cassy hadn't given much thought to what would happen after they arrived, where they would go from there. "Merrytree Cottage?" she echoed.

"If you're not happy there," he began quickly, "if you see...*something* there, we don't have to stay. We can go anywhere you want."

Cassy couldn't love him anymore than she did in that moment. She had seen ghosts throughout her life, though she didn't see them everyday. But the fact that Jack was so willing to make sure she was happy made her heart overflow. "I think Merrytree Cottage sounds delightful."

He grinned, offering her his arm. "Then, Lady St. Giles, your fishing boat awaits."

Oscar barked.

Cassy couldn't help but laugh. "A fishing boat. My mother would be green with envy."

Jack laughed too. "Well, perhaps your father inherited one from Banfield's estate."

Cassy had no idea what her father had inherited since their departure from Castle Keyvnor, but the idea of her mother traveling anywhere via fishing boat was more than amusing. "She can only hope, I'm sure."

ABOUT AVA STONE

Ava Stone is a USA Today bestselling author of Regency historical romance and college age New Adult romance. Whether in the 19th Century or the 21st, her books explore deep themes but with a light touch. A single mother, Ava lives outside Raleigh NC, but she travels extensively, always looking for inspiration for new stories and characters in the various locales she visits.

～

You can subscribe to Ava's newsletter HERE.

Connect With Ava Stone

www.avastoneauthor.com
ava@avastoneauthor.com

ALSO BY AVA STONE

~

REGENCY SEASONS SERIES